S0-CFJ-479

"I don't suppose you'd be accommodating, Nyree?"

Reid continued without waiting for an answer. "The unfortunate thing about women is that one needs them from time to time."

"How dare you!" Nyree gasped. "You're making me the object of your cynicism toward women simply because I happen to be on hand. That's about as low as any man can go in my book!"

"That's not entirely true," Reid broke in. "It occurred to me before this that I'd like to make love with you. I've often thought of what it would be like to have that magnificent, lithe body naked beneath my hands...."

"Stop!" Nyree whispered. "We barely know each other."

"I think we know each other rather well." Reid spoke tantalizingly slow as his gaze connected with hers. "But if what I was thinking hasn't occurred to you..."

"No!" Nyree snapped, realizing as she did that she lied.

LINDSAY ARMSTRONG married an accountant from New Zealand and settled down—if you can call it that—in Australia. A coast-to-coast camping trip later, they moved to a six-hundred-acre mixed grain property, which they eventually abandoned to the mice, leeches and blackflies. Then, after a winning career at the track with an untried trotter, purchased "mainly because he had blue eyes," they opted for a more conventional family life with their five children in Brisbane, where Lindsay now writes.

Books by Lindsay Armstrong

HARLEQUIN PRESENTS
559—MELT A FROZEN HEART
607—ENTER MY JUNGLE
806—SAVED FROM SIN
871—FINDING OUT
887—LOVE ME NOT
927—AN ELUSIVE MISTRESS
951—SURRENDER MY HEART
983—STANDING ON THE OUTSIDE
1039—THE SHADOW OF MOONLIGHT
1071—RELUCTANT WIFE

HARLEQUIN ROMANCE
2443—SPITFIRE
2497—MY DEAR INNOCENT
2582—PERHAPS LOVE
2653—DON'T CALL IT LOVE
2785—SOME SAY LOVE
2876—THE HEART OF THE MATTER
2893—WHEN THE NIGHT GROWS COLD

Don't miss any of our special offers. Write to us at the following address for information on our newest releases.

Harlequin Reader Service
901 Fuhrmann Blvd., P.O. Box 1397, Buffalo, NY 14240
Canadian address: P.O. Box 603,
Fort Erie, Ont. L2A 5X3

LINDSAY ARMSTRONG

when you leave me

Harlequin Books

TORONTO • NEW YORK • LONDON
AMSTERDAM • PARIS • SYDNEY • HAMBURG
STOCKHOLM • ATHENS • TOKYO • MILAN

Harlequin Presents first edition August 1988
ISBN 0-373-11095-2

Original hardcover edition published in 1987
by Mills & Boon Limited

CHAPTER ONE

AT THE time, Nyree Westbrook treated the incident with angry contempt. It was only later that she was to acknowledge the hand of fate in her life.

It all happened so quickly. One minute she was tramping through hot, silent bush across a beautiful island, an island she was being paid to visit—the next, she breasted a small rise and came upon two people, a man and a girl, engaged in an unequal struggle.

She stopped abruptly, in time to hear the girl say in a strangled whisper, 'Please don't . . . not here . . .' And to see that the young man was forcibly trying to open her blouse. It was hard to see what the difference in their ages was, if any, not at all hard to see that the girl wasn't going to win. And by the time all this had sunk in, virtually in the blink of an eyelid, the contested blouse flew open, spraying little buttons into the bush.

Nyree took immediate action. She strode up to the pair, put her hand on the man's shoulder and pushed him backwards.

As it happened, she needn't have bothered because, from nowhere it seemed, another man had appeared on the scene, a taller, older man and with one large hand he caught the offender's shoulder in a vice-like grip, swung him away from the girl then let go.

Some confusion followed. The young man fell over his own feet and ended up sitting on the ground

5

ignominiously while the girl clutched her blouse together, muttered something incomprehensible and dashed away down the path.

Nyree watched her departing back and flying hair wryly for a moment before turning her attention to the young man who had scrambled unsteadily to his feet with a mingled expression of angry incredulity and wariness. He glanced from Nyree to the other man, opened his mouth to speak but obviously thought better of it and prepared to depart himself.

But the tall stranger spoke with a soft drawl that was curiously cutting. 'Have you ever considered trying gentle persuasion rather than brute force, my friend?'

'Have you ever considered minding your own business?' the young man said sneeringly, turning back mid-stride.

'Seeing people overpowered in public is anyone's business, especially a man overcoming a girl.' The contempt in that soft voice was unmistakable and the young man went redder. 'But just in case you didn't realise you *were* open to public scrutiny, I thought you might like to know for future reference that your technique is incredibly crude.'

It was plain for Nyree to see the dilemma this advice caused the recipient of it. He clenched his hands into fists and stuck out his jaw. But his tormentor merely regarded him coolly and with the unmistakable confidence of a bigger man in every respect. Discretion won the day.

Nyree watched him leave with undignified haste.

'What a coward,' she said. 'He'd have loved to punch you on the nose.'

'I don't punch easily.'

'So I observed. Incidentally, your advice was very well meant, I'm sure, but just a little suspect, I thought.'

The man raised an eyebrow and for the first time Nyree realised he carried a golf club in one hand. He also favoured her with a dispassionate look before replying and later Nyree was to wonder why she hadn't felt the hand of fate then. She did in fact feel strangely conscious of her surroundings, of the blue, clear sky above, the heat of the sun on her back and her arms, the sand of the track in her shoes, of the silvery green leaves and amber-yellow, plump bottlebrush blooms of the tree beside them.

Then he said drily, 'Suspect in what way—is it an Amazon I have the pleasure of addressing?' He looked her up and down pointedly.

Nyree stiffened, but briefly, for this taunt wasn't new to her. She had more or less learnt to live with the fact that she was five foot eleven in her bare feet and built to match with generous breasts—someone had once said luscious, and gone on to describe her hips as magnificent. Her own appraisal of her figure drew more satisfaction from her trim, taut waistline, long legs and slender hands and feet. And only occasionally was she called to draw upon her father's wisdom in relation to her figure . . . 'You could have been short and fat or tall and skinny and round-shouldered, but in fact you're perfectly proportioned, and that's what counts,' he had said.

She grimaced because at that moment her perfect proportions—if that was true—were hidden beneath a shapeless but cool shirt pulled out of the waistband of her oldest jeans, now baggy with wear themselves. And her long brown hair was plaited into a pigtail and tied with a ribbon but probably coming adrift, she guessed. She also carried a long gnarled piece of driftwood she had picked up on the beach and used as a walking-stick—perhaps the tag of Amazon wasn't so unkind, she mused wryly, but talk about the pot calling the kettle black!

Half a lifetime of being taller than most of her sex, and as tall as most men she knew, had invested her with an inbuilt measuring mechanism, and she could say without fear of contradiction that this man was himself at least six foot three. He also, she noted, had thick, dark hair and a pair of deep blue eyes and some lines beside his mouth which invested him with a world-weary rather cynical look; he was tanned, and beneath much more reputable jeans than hers and a grey sports shirt he looked to be supremely fit and streamlined. Finally, he appeared to be in his late thirties.

'Quite finished?' he asked as her scrutiny returned to his face.

'Quite.' Nyree shrugged and turned to go herself.

'You haven't answered my question,' he said.

She hesitated and turned back.

'Suspect in what way?' he reminded her with irony.

'Well, it almost sounded as if you were advising him to lure girls into the bush with sweet words and a gentle touch—a different *technique* but the same end result in mind.'

'Only a misguided feminist would think of that,' he

murmured. 'Or someone who was herself cynical of men because she'd ... er ... got her fingers burnt once.'

Nyree coloured faintly but held his blue gaze steadily and opened her mouth to speak but he forestalled her.

'What would your advice to him have been, as a matter of interest?'

Nyree closed her mouth and wondered briefly if she had allowed her cynicism to speak for her. This was an annoying thought although more annoying to have this strange man detect it. 'I . . .' She grimaced.

'Perhaps you'd have preferred to advise the girl?' he said then with a glinting look of mockery. 'Stay away from men, my dear. They're big and bad and they bite . . .'

'If you've quite finished enjoying yourself at my expense, I'll leave,' Nyree said crisply, and swung on her heel.

But he fell into step beside her and at her irate look, said blandly, 'It seems we're going the same way. I'd just found my ball when I came across that lovers' tiff.'

'Who's to say it was a lovers' tiff?' Nyree queried tartly.

'Oh, I think it was. When I was playing the third hole they strolled across the green hand in hand.'

'Are you trying to say now that she led him on? That she wasn't entitled to resent being leapt upon in the bush and made love to or . . .'

'There is a theory,' he drawled, breaking in, 'that women don't know what they're going to enjoy until they've tried it.'

'Beside a public pathway?' she said quizzically. 'You must know some strange women!'

He laughed at her. 'Quick with your tongue as well, I see, fair Amazon. But I didn't say *I* subscribed to that theory.'

'You amaze me,' Nyree said coldly.

'Look,' he stopped walking and put a hand on her arm, 'I'm a little tired of this. I don't believe any woman should be forced into anything. If I did I should hardly have intervened then, but what I find strange is that, having done the right thing—and you do believe it was the right thing, don't you? After all you were doing the same.'

'I . . . yes . . .'

'What I find strange then, is that you *still*, you misguided feminists, find cause to quibble!'

'I'm *not* a misguided feminist . . .'

'Then what is the problem?' he said softly. 'Are you harbouring a burning sense of resentment because no man has ever invited you into the bushes to make love to you? Sometimes one's resentments express themselves twistedly.'

Nyree gasped. '*You* . . .'

But he only smiled gently at her, his blue eyes quite genuinely amused apparently.

'I . . .' She ground her teeth.

'Don't say it,' he advised mildly. 'Incidentally, we're almost on the golf course and I propose to continue my game. Care to join me? We could share the clubs.'

'*Join* you!' she said disbelievingly.

He shrugged. 'It's a good way of working off one's frustrations.'

Nyree's lips parted, but she closed her eyes, counted to five and stalked away.

She remained burningly angry all the way across the golf course and until she came to the beach, where she found Simon involved in a sandcastle competition under the supervision of the resort nanny. And after admiring his half-completed castle and that of his new-found friend, Dean, she decided they were still well occupied, so she walked up to the Sand Bar, ordered a long, cool drink and took it over to a table outside where she could see the kids.

Only then did she find herself relaxing and even reviewing the incident with a tinge of—could it be remorse? Well, he had a point, she mused. If I'm cynical and bitter about men, it's not without cause, but there's a difference between being wary and cautious, and ridiculously paranoid on the subject—or there should be. Have I fallen into that trap, she wondered a little sadly. Because of one man and what he did to me?

On the other hand, she thought then—and felt some of her resentment return—to taunt me with being frustrated and . . . that was quite hateful! I wouldn't be at all surprised if he *is* a male chauvinist despite feeling duty-bound to rescue distressed little girls. No, I wouldn't be surprised at all!

But finally, being a practical person, not to mention unaware of the hand of fate, she decided to forget the incident. Which was not so hard to do, seated on a tree-shaded terrace watching the sea dancing in the afternoon sunlight and with nothing more arduous to do than take care of and entertain one ten-year-old boy, who was an extremely well-mannered little boy, for all that he was far too quiet for a child of that age.

Nyree narrowed her eyes and watched the *Victory*, which plied the waters between Yeppoon and Great Keppel Island, sail away towards the mainland with a consignment of happy day trippers, and she recalled how it had come about, this paid holiday.

Four years ago after graduating from university, she had looked around for a way of augmenting her income as a teacher. Not that she had been badly paid at the private school where she taught senior English, nor was she particularly poor. But she'd invested the inheritance her father had left her into an apartment and decided to keep the boat that her father had also left her. Yet, much as she loved the boat and the happy memories of all the marvellous times they'd had on it, the plain facts of it were that it cost money to maintain, money to run, money to moor for quite long stretches at a time. So, for the privilege of spending a few weeks and as many weekends a year as she could manage on board, she had enlisted with an employment agency that provided permanent and temporary home help.

During term-time she was restricted to baby-sitting in the evenings, but during the school holidays she often moved into a household to take care of the children or sometimes the elderly—or sometimes just the dog and the cat and the pot-plants while the owners took a holiday. Over the years she had established 'regulars' but, perhaps most important, she'd established a reputation with the agency for reliability and the ability to cope with all sorts of unforeseen crises, unruly children and pets, asthmatics and other problems. She had also become friendly with the head of the agency, Gwen Foster.

But when, two weeks ago, Gwen had rung and asked if she was free over the school holidays, she'd hesitated for a moment, then said cautiously that she was, but that she was actually feeling rather tired ...

'Then this will be perfect for you, Nyree!' Gwen had enthused over the phone. 'Two weeks on Great Keppel with only one child to look after, all expenses paid—what more could you ask for?'

Nyree had blinked. 'Keppel?' she had said rather dazedly. 'You mean the "Get Wrecked" island? Off Rockhampton?'

'The same,' Gwen had said happily. 'I believe it's beautiful: marvellous beaches, fabulous bush walks—you can hire sailing boats, and as for getting wrecked, I have the greatest faith in you, Nyree.'

Nyree had smiled faintly. The 'Get Wrecked on Great Keppel' advertising campaign had been extremely successful and, at least in Queensland, the term had almost passed into the local folklore. What it meant, she gathered, was that as well as a beautiful island to play on during the day, the nightlife was well-developed too. But still she had hesitated. 'Tell me about the child, Gwen.'

'Ten years old,' Gwen had become businesslike, 'comes from a broken home and has since lost his mother. He's presently in his aunt's care and they—his aunt, his uncle and his father—were going to take him on this holiday, but due to a succession of unfortunate coincidences none of them can get away now. Um ... the aunt has broken a bone in her foot and can only hobble about, the father is overseas on business and has been unavoidably detained—everything has just gone wrong for them in other words, and they're quite upset about it, especially as the child was apparently looking forward to the holiday. There is a possibility the Inchwoods, that's the aunt and uncle, could join you for the second week if her foot heals well enough. What do you think?'

Nyree had considered. 'But how will he take to a stranger?'

'Well he must be a fairly well-adjusted kid,' Gwen had said, 'because he's at boarding school, a weekly boarder. But they're certainly very concerned to find a suitable companion and I can vouch for *them* to an extent because I've supplied them with permanent staff several times who've found them most satisfactory and generous to work for.'

'Rich, I gather?'

'I gather so. Nyree, I have no one on my books I could recommend more highly than you, my dear, and I've taken the liberty of supplying Mrs Inchwood with your references . . .

One week later, Nyree was boarding a jet for Rockhampton with Simon Matthews, aged ten.

He was quite tall for his age with straight fair hair, very blue eyes and an undoubtedly English accent. He was also, Nyree decided by the time they'd transferred from the jet at Rockhampton to a Twin Otter, very reserved. In fact she had hardly got a word out of him. Which concerned her not only because they'd be spending a fortnight in each other's company but also because she got the impression the reserve was something more than a shy child might show in the company of a stranger. She couldn't quite say why this impression took hold of her so strongly, and at first she dismissed it as plain shyness. It was, after all, an odd situation, being sent on holiday with a paid companion. Then she decided there was a bolted-down quality to Simon Matthews, and this was reinforced when they flew over Keppel and banked sharply for the descent, and Simon swallowed visibly and gritted his teeth and broke out into a sweat.

'It's all right,' she said gently. 'We'll make it.'

But instead of being reassured, he had blushed and she had guessed he was ashamed of showing his fear. She had found then, for the first time, that she was unusually moved by this little boy.

She'd found out later, over the next few days, that Simon clamped down on most emotions, that his greatest show of enthusiasm was a faint smile, and she couldn't help wondering why he had been looking forward to this holiday so much so that his relations had been spurred into providing it at all costs.

She also discovered that he suffered from nightmares. One night he woke up and she heard him, through the open door between their rooms, twisting restlessly in bed. She had gone in to find him sitting up in bed with tears on his cheeks, looking frightened and very young and alone.

'Simon? What is it?'

'Nothing.' He scrubbed at his eyes furiously.

'Would you like a cup of coffee? It's probably not good for you but if you've had a bad dream, I reckon we could make an exception.'

His relief that she wasn't going to press him for details was pitifully evident, and she made him a weak cup of coffee and one for herself, and sat on the end of his bed discussing their plans for the next day. He fell asleep soon afterwards and as she tucked him in she was conscious of a burning resolve somehow to break through that reserve, and give him the best holiday of his life.

And I think I've partly succeeded, she mused. He's certainly opened up a lot, he's even made a friend. But he still hasn't ever once mentioned his aunt and uncle or his father.

She thought about this as she finished her drink and then found her thoughts taking another direction towards a tall man with very blue eyes and one who, she realised regretfully, wasn't going to be so easy to forget after all. And not only because there was the distinct possibility she would run into him again—the resort wasn't full by any means—but also because by an uncanny trick of fate he had managed to expose a weak spot in her armour, a tendency to ridiculous cynicism. What was worse perhaps, though, was how this exposé had opened up all those painful memories. Memories of being in love and being duped, of being too blinded by love or passion or whatever to see Brad's weakness, to be taken in by his lies. Memories of self-disgust that she could have been such a naïve fool, memories of aching loneliness . . .

'Nyree? Guess what! I won a prize for my castle!'

With a start of relief, Nyree came out of her reverie and she ruffled Simon's fair hair briefly, admired his prize and bought him a Coke. Then she looked at her watch and suggested they go up to their rooms for their evening ritual before getting ready for dinner. Simon agreed happily.

The month was June—mid-winter in Australia—but on the Tropic of Capricorn the days were warm and balmy although night closed in swiftly and brought a sparkling chill to the air. It was cooling down perceptibly as she and Simon stepped out on to her veranda which overlooked the beach, and some feathery clouds had partly obscured the sinking sun with the result that the water stretching away towards the rugged outline of the mainland was a delicate aquamarine shade, tinged faintly with pink. And when the sun broke through the cloud, it laid a shimmering path of golden light on the sea.

Nyree and Simon watched fascinated as they did every evening, knowing what was to come but still capable of being enthralled by the beauty of it. For when the sun finally left the sky, it left the horizon a pure, fiery orange fading to lemon and darkening blue, and it left the water, in those minutes before darkness fell completely, a luminous cornflower-blue darkening to violet.

Nyree often thought if she saw it painted she wouldn't believe it, and she wondered if it was the dry, dusty country of inland Australia that stretched back from Rockhampton that accounted for it, but mostly she was simply enchanted.

Gwen Foster had been right about Great Keppel, it was beautiful; for the most part untouched virgin bush alive with bird-life, native fauna and fringed by no less than seventeen glorious beaches. And, while the resort accommodation was modern and comfortable, it was surrounded by flowering trees and lawns.

'Well,' she said to Simon as the last light left the sky, 'time to get ready for dinner.'

'OK,' he answered cheerfully, adding, 'I'm starving!'

Nyree grinned. 'You always are!'

Dinner at Keppel started at six-thirty. At ten past six, Nyree stepped out of the shower, dried herself and donned a short, silky yellow robe, and left the en suite bathroom to get dressed.

She had closed out the chill night air and closed the curtains, and the room was warm and the greens and yellows used in the decor were glowing softly in the lamplight. She closed the interconnecting door to Simon's room and smiled as she heard him whistling in the shower.

Clothes required for dinner were smart casual and hers were laid out on the bed: a pair of cream linen pants, an amber blouse and a loose cream jacket with square shoulders and no lapels. Honey-brown polished leather shoes with small wooden heels and a matching leather belt completed the outfit. But just as she was about to start dressing someone knocked on the outer door.

She frowned, put her lacy underwear down again, tightened the belt of her robe and went to open it.

'*You* . . .!' she gasped disbelievingly.

'Well, well,' the tall man on the doorstep drawled, 'if it isn't our Amazon. Look,' he turned to someone behind him and said impatiently, 'there's got to be some mistake, and if you don't mind, I've had a long, frustrating day and I'm getting fairly annoyed.'

There was no doubt he looked it too with his mouth now clamped in a hard straight line and those lines beside it deeply scored.

The person behind him proved to be a staff member, a girl from Reception, and she said a shade nervously, 'There's no mistake, sir. This is Miss Westbrook and . . .'

'*This* is Miss Westbrook?' Those hard blue eyes flicked to Nyree and seemed to scorch her. 'If that's so,' the man said gratingly to her then, 'would you kindly tell me what the hell you were doing tramping the island on your *own* when Simon was nowhere to be found?'

'Si . . . Simon?' Nyree stammered from sheer shock.

'Er . . .' the girl from Reception interposed.

But he ignored her and said savagely to Nyree, 'Go on, I'm waiting.'

Nyree took a breath and her nostrils flared. She said precisely, '*I'm* in charge of Simon and I've no idea what your interest in him is, nor do I have to explain my actions to you—nor do I intend to until *you* explain yourself!' She glared at him and folded her arms defiantly over her breasts as if she was physically prepared to defend Simon from him which she was at that moment.

'Explain myself?' the man said almost gently but lingeringly and with so much mockery Nyree longed to hit him. 'I merely happen to be his father.'

Later, Nyree was to curse herself for what happened

then, for what she said. But at the time she felt a simmering sense of resentment, not only at what she had undergone already at the hands of this man, whether she had been in the right or the wrong, but also at the injustice she felt on Simon's behalf.

She said, 'Well, I only have your word for that, and if you are his father, there are some things you appear to be criminally ignorant of!'

'Er ... Miss Westbrook,' the girl from Reception said hastily, 'we have a telex from TAA Brisbane for you.' She flourished a piece of paper. 'From a Gwen Foster. Would you like to read it?'

The telex was uncompromising. Gwen had sent a plain message ... *Simon's father Reid Matthews arriving Keppel today. Take further instructions from him. Signed: Gwen Foster.*

Nyree read it and re-read it. Then she lifted her green eyes and studied both Reid Matthews and the girl and said drily, 'I suppose I can't leave until tomorrow morning?'

There was a short, uncomfortable silence at least for the girl from Reception. 'No, and as a matter of fact both flights out tomorrow are fully booked . . .' she said awkwardly.

Reid Matthews interrupted her. 'Thank you, I'll take it from here. These are,' he gestured, 'two separate rooms?'

'Oh yes, sir, Mr Matthews. With an interleading door but quite self-contained. You can lock the door . . .'

'I'll remind Miss Westbrook of that,' he said flatly. '*If* there's any chance of rustling up my luggage tomorrow morning I'd be most grateful,' he added.

The girl swallowed. 'We do really apologise for that, Mr Matthews. I've telexed both Brisbane and Rockhampton. Er . . . the shop is closed but I could arrange for them to open up . . .'

'That's all right, I can manage for tonight but thank you.' He smiled at her. Whereupon she blushed, looked flustered and took herself off.

Nyree turned away in disgust and marched back into the room. She heard the door close and turned round to confront Simon's father. Suddenly the resemblance between the two of them struck her and rather took the wind out of her sails. When you knew what to look for, they had the same very blue eyes, same mouths, and although Simon was fair, the same shaped heads.

Unfortunately, the lead passed to Reid Matthews while she was thinking these thoughts.

'I'm waiting for your explanation, Miss Westbrook,' he said with cold determination, and added, 'As you might have gathered, my luggage has been lost in transit, but for your further edification, it was only touch and go whether I got on the flight from Brisbane this morning—there was a very late cancellation. Then when I arrived here, no one could find you and Simon so I spent some time twiddling my thumbs before I decided to have a game of golf. I'm telling you all this, Miss Westbrook, so that you'll understand I'm fast losing patience.'

Nyree narrowed her green eyes. 'Dear me,' she said, 'how very trying your day has been.' She looked at him contemptuously and went on coolly. 'But it's quite simple. They have a resort nanny here who supervises children between the ages of three and thirteen, but up until today, Simon hasn't been interested. This morning, though, he met a boy of his own age who suggested they take part in this afternoon's activities which included a sandcastle competition . . .'

'He wasn't building sandcastles on the beach when I was looking for him,' Simon's father interrupted.

'There were also to be beach games for the older ones,' Nyree said deliberately. 'They could have been far up the other end at the time but I can assure you that while you—were relieving your serious *frustrations* on the golf course, Simon was building sandcastles on the beach in front of the Sand Bar. I can also assure you he would have been properly supervised at all times, otherwise I would not have left him. But perhaps you'd care to check with Simon? Or the nanny? I'm sure we could produce her for—an *interrogation*.'

The atmosphere between them crackled with tension.

'You have a very cutting tongue, my dear,' he said, his lips barely moving. 'Not at all the sort of person I would want to be looking after my son.'

'And you, Mr Matthews,' Nyree said sweetly, 'have a charming son which I find rather incredible, having now met you. But then again perhaps it's not so incredible, because he obviously spends most of his life away from you.'

Two things caused Nyree to break off. Reid Matthews went white under his tan and Simon knocked on the interleading door.

Nyree flinched and wondered briefly what had got

into her. It was really none of her business *but* . . . She bit her lip and walked over to the door and opened it.

'Oh! Sorry,' Simon said. 'I thought you'd be ready. I'll wait.' And he started to turn away.

But Nyree, conscious for the first time of her state of undress, murmured, 'No . . . uh . . . Simon, there's someone here to see you. Come in.'

Simon came and his eyes widened and he stopped short. 'Dad! What are you doing here?'

Reid Matthews suddenly looked quite different, Nyree noticed. There was no sign of anger or sardonic mockery but she also noticed that as he smiled at his son, his eyes were curiously acute. 'I got back from Europe earlier than expected after all so I've come to share your holiday. Do you mind?'

'No,' Simon said politely then all but took Nyree's breath away by adding, 'We were doing fine on our own, though. Nyree's just tops—for a girl. She's taught me to sail catamarans and lots of things. We were really enjoying ourselves, so you didn't have to rush back.'

The silence that greeted his words was almost deafening until Nyree closed her mouth with a click. She wrested her gaze from Simon, who was now looking his most reserved, to his father, with her eyes wide and questioning as she wondered dazedly whether she'd *imagined* it or whether Simon had truly given his father a complete brush-off.

The murderous glint of anger in those blue eyes that clashed with hers over Simon's head told her that she had not. Why it should be squarely directed at her was not terribly hard to fathom either. In her blind hostility and resentment earlier, just before Simon had knocked, she had obviously scored a direct hit. There had to be acute trauma in this father-son relationship and she had unwittingly, well, almost unwittingly, unearthed it; but in a manner . . . Oh hell, she thought, why didn't I keep my mouth shut?

But he was nothing if not resourceful, Simon's father. After that one scorching glance, his expression was bland now and just a touch rueful as he regarded his son and said lightly, 'I'll do my best to keep it enjoyable, Simon. Why don't we let . . . Nyree get dressed, by the way?' Again that blue gaze flicked to her over Simon's head but this time it effectively stripped her naked beneath the flimsy robe so that she coloured and could have killed herself, but more so him. 'We could discuss this over dinner. Lead on, young man.'

But Simon stood his ground stubbornly. 'Discuss what? You're not going to send her home, are you? Now you're here?'

For the life of her Nyree couldn't resist retaliating, although she regretted it immediately. She flashed Reid Matthews a taunting little look then closed her eyes briefly and cursed herself inwardly. How could she have?

'I . . . Simon, I would like to get dressed,' she said. 'I won't take long.'

'Take as long as you like, Nyree,' Reid drawled. 'I intend to have a shower. Come, Simon,' he said firmly, and Simon hesitated then went.

Nyree had dressed mechanically.

Now she sat in front of the wide dressing-table mirror doing her face and hair absent-mindedly. The face that stared back at her above the tailored silky amber blouse with long sleeves and fitted cuffs was a face that often captured attention. Not because it was especially beautiful, but more because her expression was generally calm, confident and serene, her eyes steady and mostly green with little brown flecks in them and with quite long lashes, and her mouth well cut. She sometimes wondered whether she had inherited the ability to look calm and confident from her mother who had died when she was very young, for her father, a ship's captain, had had an inherently different expression, rather stern and forbidding, although underneath he'd been a darling. But she'd always been thankful for the ability to mask her inner feelings, especially when they were far from calm and confident, such as when her father had died and after Brad . . .

And it was a face that somehow seemed to inspire confidence, trust and respect.

But not today, she thought, as she smoothed on moisturiser, shaped her eyebrows and applied some mascara to her lashes. She rarely bothered with lipstick and didn't tonight. No, not today . . . What an incredible sequence of events. And what difference would it have made, I wonder, if I hadn't . . . spoken rather unwisely to Reid Matthews this afternoon? But really, was it cause to dislike me *so* thoroughly, which he did before I ever mentioned Simon?

She smoothed some cream on to her long elegant hands and strapped on her rather lovely large, rectangular gold-faced watch on a brown alligator-skin band, then said softly aloud, 'Perhaps. I did . . . he *was* doing the right thing and I did take an unthinkingly unfair tilt at him. I suppose if I were to invoke misguided feminism I couldn't find a more apt example. The unfortunate thing is that men have such fragile egos, whereas they expect women to undergo far worse and come up . . . loving and smiling. For the record, so what if I *was* a touch misguided? I've been repaid with interest . . . what was probably equivalent to a butterfly bite has been revenged by a bite from a cobra . . . really, Nyree, you are getting fanciful!'

She picked up her brush and stroked her long brown hair with it. Then she drew it back with combs above her ears and stood up.

And really looked at herself in the mirror for the first time to find an errant spark of humour lighting her green eyes. For an Amazon, she couldn't help feeling she was looking rather sleek and trim in her amber blouse and well-fitting pants.

But the spark faded almost immediately, faded at the thought of Simon caught in this cross-fire. Poor kid, she thought. Then, why? Why are things like this between them? Is this the product of divorce? How close did *I* come to doing it to . . . some children . . .?

CHAPTER TWO

'IN THE light of what I now know of you, Miss Westbrook, would you consider staying on for the rest of the week?'

Nyree gasped.

Somehow or other she had got through dinner with Simon and his father but it had been strained and difficult. Simon had been withdrawn and not even hungry, and he had answered his father's questions about the holiday so far in monosyllables. To give him credit, Nyree had to admit that Reid Matthews had managed to appear unperturbed by this treatment. But when Dean had come up to the table and invited Simon to play Monopoly in the Sunset Lounge with his brothers and sisters, the sigh of relief around the table had been unheard but unmistakable.

Then Reid had suggested they go up to the lounge too, for a liqueur, and Nyree had rather helplessly accepted.

'Stay on?' she said huskily, staring down at the brandy Alexander he had bought her. She raised her green eyes at last. 'I can't see how it could work.'

'Then I'll explain,' he said with a tigerish glance. 'You've probably noticed that Simon and I have some problems, *Nyree.*'

She compressed her lips. 'I'd have been blind not to, *Mr* Matthews.'

27

'Good!' He smiled unpleasantly. 'Would you also accept that you and Simon have become friends, almost—close friends?'

'I would,' she said steadily.

'And that he's going to be very upset if you go and see me in the light of some callous monster—if he doesn't already?'

A little flame of anger lit Nyree's eyes. 'There are two things I take exception to in your reasoning, Mr Matthews,' she said tightly. 'First, that you seem to bear me a grudge for having made a friend of your son when it was only part of my job. I was employed and paid to take Simon on holiday and ensure he had a good time. The only way I could do that was to attempt to remove the barrier of two strangers flung into each other's company. And that leads on to my second point—you rather make it sound as if I've deliberately set out to alienate Simon from you, which is extremely unfair. What . . . whatever has happened between you and Simon, happened before I ever met him and is none of my business, nor did he ever confide in me, so . . .'

'You made some remarks earlier in the evening, Miss Westbrook, which led me to think otherwise. You accused me of being criminally ignorant. You also flashed me a look of unmistakable triumph when Simon showed such preference for your company.'

Nyree took a breath and said, 'Ah. Thank you for mentioning that, because it puts me in mind of point three. What I said, and looked, came out in the heat of the moment—not that I retract what I said because I have quite some experience of children and it was obvious to me, in a general way, that Simon,' she spread her hands and shrugged, 'was not a very happy little boy. But the *way* I said it was the result of a certain, shall we say ... inability, *we* have of being able to see eye to eye, Mr Matthews.' She stared at him defiantly.

'And the look?' he said softly. 'That triumphant look, Miss Westbrook?' His blue gaze was laced with mockery.

Nyree gritted her teeth and replied equally softly. 'If you go about undressing women with your eyes, Mr Matthews, you shouldn't be surprised when they retaliate by any means to hand.'

The corners of his mouth twitched then he grinned wryly and said, 'Touché!' But he added almost immediately, 'So we're back to square one? That hoary old subject which was the cause of our original—how did you put it?—ah yes, our original inability to see eye to eye. Well, for the record, perhaps I have been a bit unfair to you. Unfortunately I'm a little allergic to—I was going to say to misguided feminists but I'll rephrase, overbearing—no ... uh ...'

'Don't bother,' Nyree said furiously. 'This is an impossible conversation and what you're asking me to do is impossible. So if you'll excuse me I'll remove my overbearing, feminist, not to mention Amazonlike person from your presence!'

'Oh,' he drawled, 'I've revised my opinion on the Amazon tag. Yes,' he went on lazily, 'from closer inspection of your ... person, I think rather spectacularly gorgeous would be a better way to describe ... it.'

It was years since Nyree had blushed as brightly

and at the same time had a whole host of emotions jostle for supremacy—he had to be the most unpleasant man she had ever met—how *dared* he sit there observing her amusedly and dispassionately after . . . As if it was any of his business to be assessing her figure! For that matter, how dared she be blushing like a schoolgirl!

'You're insufferable,' she said in a low, husky voice. 'You're the worst kind of male chauvinist I've ever met, despite what you did this morning. You're also impossibly arrogant and . . . and if I do despise men I'm heartily happy about it at this moment!' The last bit slipped out unwittingly, but she held her head high and glared at him, then started to rise.

'Well,' he observed and watched her quizzically, 'that certainly clears the air. Why don't you relax now and perhaps we could get down to brass tacks.'

'Brass—I just don't believe the gall of you!' Nyree raged. 'What brass tacks? And if you ask me, the air is much clearer away from you.'

'I *meant*—we've sorted out that I'm the kind of man you detest most and that you're the kind of woman whom . . . I tend to steer clear of other than in a business context. So we understand each other, wouldn't you say?' He turned away as he spoke and signalled the bar tender to order two fresh drinks. Then he turned back and said, 'As for the brass tacks, I'm desperate to get closer to my son, Miss Westbrook. Circumstance has dealt him a cruel blow and I'll do anything in my power to rectify that. Anything,' he repeated and there was no malice or mockery in his eyes or voice, just grim, bleak determination. 'You,' he went on, 'have worked a small miracle with Simon and I have to acknowledge that at first it galled me. I've tried . . . well, it's pretty obvious I've tried and failed whereas in the space of a week you've got closer to him than anyone. Now,' he paused briefly, 'I could dress this up with apologies, but perhaps it would be more honest to say, for Simon's sake, would you be prepared to bury the hatchet for the rest of this week and . . . work *with* me to help him?'

'I . . .' Nyree had stood up but she sank back slowly. 'I . . .' she said confusedly and couldn't go on.

'I realise I'll be *using* you—to put it quite plainly— to raise myself in his estimation by . . . gaining your approval, currying favour if you like, but . . .' He stopped, picked up his drink then put it down untasted, and shrugged. 'Somehow I have to break through this wall he's erected between us. I'm the only one he has left—for that matter, he's all I have.'

Nyree had been staring at the blue runner on the bar but she lifted her eyes at last and stared into his blue ones, and could not mistake the shadow of torment in them.

'How—did it happen?' she asked abruptly, at last.

'His mother left me because she was pregnant by another man—so she told me. When she died eighteen months ago, her parents contacted me and revealed the truth. Simon was my son.'

Nyree's eyes were appalled. 'And you never guessed?' she whispered.

His mouth hardened. 'I won't bore you with the details but no. I laid eyes on him for the first time when he was eight and a half. I . . . shall never forgive myself for believing her, for . . .' he sighed suddenly and looked weary, 'believing her, for . . .'

He broke off and the lines beside his mouth were so harshly scored that he looked suddenly weary beyond words and deeply unhappy.

'I'll never forgive myself,' he said very quietly, 'it's as simple as that.' He picked up his glass.

'I . . . well, I can't go tomorrow, by the sound of it,' Nyree said.

'You could take a boat.'

'Don't you want me to stay now?'

'Of course I do. I just don't want you to act as if I've kept you here against your will.'

Nyree favoured him with a smouldering glance.

'Well, it's not going to work, is it, if you're going to act as if you're under duress?' he said impatiently.

'All I said was that I can't go tomorrow!'

'And all I'm asking you to do,' he countered, 'is put your heart and soul into it *if* you're going to do it.'

'*All?*' She looked at him ironically. 'You're a hard man to please, Mr Matthews,' she murmured.

'So I've been told. Well?'

Nyree bit her lip and wondered how she could possibly survive a week in his company. But the sound of laughter came from the table across the room where the children were playing Monopoly and she glanced over at Simon, and was lost.

'Yes,' she said with an inward sigh, 'I'll stay.'

She was destined never to know his reaction because a purring voice said beside them then, 'Why, Reid! Here you are. I was wondering what had happened to you.'

Reid turned then stood up. 'Hello Amy,' he said. 'This is Nyree Westbrook—Amy Kelly.'

Nyree murmured 'How do you do,' and noted that Amy Kelly was beautiful with gleaming fair hair, smooth pale skin and a good figure. She would be at least a head shorter than I am, Nyree calculated, and about twenty-two.

'Not another friend!' Amy said quizzically. 'Isn't it a small world—I was just saying that to Reid this afternoon when we bumped into each other. He was looking quite demented,' she confided artlessly to Nyree. 'He'd not only lost his little boy but the nanny too. Did you find them, darling?' She swivelled her grey eyes to Reid and they sparkled with amusement—and unabashed interest.

'Yes, but . . .'

'I'm the nanny, actually,' Nyree said and stood up.

Amy was only slightly taken back, but Reid looked at them both standing side by side and a glint of something like humour lit his eyes, causing Nyree to wonder swiftly if he was going to say something about the long and the tall and the short . . .

But it was Amy who spoke with an eager little rush. 'Does that mean that you're free after all this evening, Reid? A group of us are going over to the Wreck Bar for the disco . . .'

'I'm sorry,' Reid broke in, 'but I'd like to be with Simon tonight. I've also had a fairly long day and I doubt if I'm up to a disco.'

'That I don't believe,' Amy murmured with a provocative glance up and down the tall, strong length of him.

Reid Matthews grinned and the flash of white teeth against his tan and the glint in his blue, blue eyes, added to the big taut body, made a picture that was undeniably extremely good-looking. But Nyree was staring at him with something like disbelief in her eyes and she was thinking, he's enjoying this—how could you not be nauseated—so that's how he likes his women! No wonder he doesn't like me . . .

'I'd be happy to put Simon to bed for you, Mr Matthews,' she said coolly but with a certain lack of forethought, she realised almost immediately.

'Not at all, Miss Westbrook,' he replied just as coolly. 'We'll do it together.'

Nyree shrugged and turned away, leaving him to deal with Amy who had followed their exchange and Reid's sudden change of face with a tiny frown knitting her forehead.

Then Amy wafted away and Nyree looked up at him, and having had a few moments to remind herself that she had agreed to his—terms—it took her a moment to think of an alternative word for dictates— she forestalled whatever he might have been about to say by saying herself, briskly, 'Sorry—that just slipped out. Probably by tomorrow I'll have got used to the . . .'

'Idea of being on friendly terms with me of all people?' he offered with irony.

'Yes,' she said flatly. 'By the way, talking about tomorrow, Simon and I were planning to hike over to Leeke's homestead with a picnic lunch.'

'Sounds like a good idea to me,' he said after a moment's thought.

'Then how would it be if I took myself off to bed now so that I can polish up my act for tomorrow,' despite herself a wry little smile twisted Nyree's lips, 'and you could break the news to Simon? That I'm staying, I mean, not . . .' She broke off.

'I presumed that's what you meant, but why don't *you* have a night off? I don't suppose you've had a chance to sample the night life yet.'

'Nor do I propose to,' she said quietly, and suddenly discovered she felt extremely weary herself. It had, after all, been a long, complicated day and it was obviously going to be a long, complicated week. 'Please . . .' She made a curiously helpless little gesture and looked down.

He surprised her. He put a hand on her chin and tilted her head back and studied her face in silence for a moment then he said, 'How old are you, Nyree—and please call me Reid.

'Twenty-six,' she said huskily. 'Why?'

'That's what I thought at first, roughly, but just then you looked younger.' He smiled faintly.

'How old . . .' She stopped and bit her lip.

'Thirty-nine.' He waited for some reaction then he said musingly, 'Twenty-six,' his lips twisted ironically, 'from my distant memory of it, is rather young to be so . . . cynical, is it not?'

She moved her head and he dropped his hand. But she could think of nothing to say, she could only shrug tiredly.

And he said finally, 'All right, off you go. Goodnight.'

She immediately felt foolish as well as oddly young and unwise. A flash of hostility also came to her eyes, but she veiled it with her lashes and, murmuring goodnight, she walked away.

But, tired as she was, she still forced herself to try to

analyse that odd mixture of emotions as she got ready for bed. Mainly she decided, because she had the distinct feeling that beneath the act she and Reid Matthews planned to put on for Simon's benefit, she would still need to be well armed.

'Which means,' she murmured, staring at herself clad in a slim, pale green, silky nightgown in the mirror, 'since I'm so perceptibly a cynic—before my time, what's more—I should be sure of my ground, doesn't it? But how to do that . . . Remind myself that at the even earlier age of twenty-one, I fell in love with a man, I became his mistress and I believed every word he told me—I never dreamt he would lie to me. So, when I found out he had, I left him and I . . . walled myself up against ever being hurt like that again. But part of that wall took the form of distrusting men in general. How strange . . . because normally Nyree Westbrook is such a sane creature and the last person to believe in sweeping generalisations.'

She sighed suddenly and closed her eyes. But when I really believed that, she thought with a tremor, I'd had no experience of what . . . how vulnerable the love of a man can make you, how . . . perhaps I should be more like Amy Kelly instead of . . .

Her lashes flew up and she stared into her green eyes ruefully. And murmured, 'Oh dear, Nyree, she got to you, didn't she? But,' she answered herself, 'I'm always at a disadvantage beside short girls—I just thought I'd got over worrying about it! Why am I? Well, I'm not—not on her account, but . . . oh, hell! Go to bed, Nyree, before you get angry and unwarrantably cynical all over again!'

She fell asleep with little difficulty but woke at two o'clock feeling restless and very much alone. Rather like Simon, she reflected as she turned on to her side and slipped her hand beneath the pillow, only of course I'm too old to have nightmares about it. I just . . . wish his father hadn't come; no, I shouldn't, for Simon's sake I shouldn't. But I guess I felt more needed when there were only the two of us. And now, I've got to think of some way to bring the two of *them* together and I don't have the slightest idea how to do it . . .

But as she lay there, deliberately trying to relax and go back to sleep, she was suddenly assailed by the memory of love . . . Of how it felt to sleep in a man's arms and many more memories until she sat up at last and said softly, 'Damn! Damn you, Reid Matthews. Of all people why did you have to be Simon's father and why did it have to be you I said what I did to this morning? Nine other men out of ten . . . oh!' She flung the covers back exasperatedly and got up to make herself a cup of tea. But by five-thirty she was still awake and by six she gave up the struggle. She pulled on her swimming-costume, added a warm jumper and jeans, collected a towel and strode out to go for a tramp along the beach and a swim.

Several hours later, she eyed the very steep hill they had just started to climb and found herself sincerely regretting her excess of exercise earlier in the morning. She had walked for a couple of miles in the light of a pink and gold dawn, and swum vigorously. All of which had been fairly successful as mind-cleansing routines and not the best preparation for a cross-island hike after a rather sleepless night.

'Something wrong?' Reid Matthews queried.

'No,' she said hastily. 'I'm fine.'

But he stopped walking and so did she, reluctantly. Because he was studying her thoughtfully, her crisp white shorts and sand shoes, her long golden legs, her green T-shirt and finally her face. Then he said with his lips quirking, 'You looked at this hill with every evidence of loathing a moment ago.'

'Did I?' she murmured a little wryly. 'I can't think why.'

'Neither can I. I would have thought you were rather fit, Nyree.'

And there's no doubting *you're* extremely fit—his words caused the thought to ripple across her mind as she returned his scrutiny with inward irritation. In blue shorts and a white shirt, there was not a lot of Reid Matthews left to the imagination. So that even to me, she mused, he looks almost overpoweringly big . . . and as if this wretched hill is not a veritable mountain but a molehill.

'In fact you look almost tired,' he commented then. 'As if your early night wasn't much help after all.'

Nyree bit her lip and cursed him inwardly. He was really uncannily perceptive, this man. 'No, it wasn't,' she said shortly then added, glancing up the track, 'Oh, Simon's out of sight. Shouldn't we . . .'

But Simon's father put two fingers to his mouth and whistled piercingly, whereupon Simon hove back into view. 'There's a look-out up here!' he called down to them. 'Can I wait for you there?'

Reid gave him the thumbs-up sign and turned back to Nyree. 'Why not?'

'Why not what?'

'I think you know what I mean . . .'

'I don't,' she interrupted. 'By the way, Simon seems . . . happier this morning.' This fact had been obvious from the time they had joined forces for breakfast. Not that Simon had accorded his father anything but politeness, but he had been visibly enthusiastic about their plans for the day and rather quaintly concerned with all the arrangements such as hiring the knapsacks, organising the picnic lunches and so on. And then, when they had started out beneath a wide, clear blue sky and with the promise of a perfect day ahead, he had exhibited all the energy that ten-year-olds have in such abundance.

'Yes, he does,' Reid said steadily. 'He was . . . very relieved to know that you were staying on.

Nyree winced, which he noticed and he added, 'Well, Rome wasn't built in a day. But at least if he's in an enthusiastic frame of mind it—it might make it easier. But I'd still like to know why you didn't sleep well last night and why you were prowling the beach at the crack of dawn this morning.'

'I was not *prowling* . . . how do you know that anyway?' she demanded going rather red-faced.

He shrugged. 'I saw you from our veranda. I'm . . . let's say I'm an early riser myself.'

'I . . .' Nyree stopped and took a hold of her annoyance. 'I guess I was worried,' she said drily.

'Oh?'

'Well . . . I mean I've agreed to help you with Simon but I couldn't work out what I could actually *do*. I can't *say* much to him, I . . .'

'I don't expect you to. All I'm asking is that we

spend this week as friends and that it, as I said earlier, will hopefully allow him to be more receptive to me. It's quite simple really—and nothing for you to have spent a sleepless night over,' he said with a tinge of irony.

Nyree breathed deeply and lowered her lashes to escape that blue inquisitor's gaze. She said tonelessly, 'OK. Shall we . . . get going?'

But he didn't move, just regarded her silently until her nerves began to thrum like taut wires, and she said exasperatedly, 'What is it now?'

He chewed his lip maddeningly. 'If I didn't know you better, I'd say you look like the victim of a hangover, taut and aching and . . .'

'You don't know me at all so how can you—I mean I'm not,' she retorted. 'But there's no way you could . . .'

'Oh,' he said lazily, 'I'd be very surprised if you were.'

'Then why . . . Look,' she said crossly, 'I may offend your ideas of feminine proportions, in fact your whole concept of the feminine ideal, but I am human!'

'Are you . . . boasting of your hangovers, Nyree?' he queried gently.

'No! But I have had one . . . well . . .'

'The very rare, very mild one and only before you learnt your limitations?'

Nyree ground her teeth. 'Why do you persist in making me feel like some kind of freak?' she flashed at him.

'I think this particular—inability to see eye to eye is of your making,' he said musingly, then grinned at her suddenly. 'Also that it's wise to choose one's ground to have a fight on.'

'You brought the subject up!'

'Ah, but if it had been the other way around I'd have given this . . . bout a miss.'

Nyree experienced that unpleasant sinking feeling common to those who know they've taken up the wrong cause, been unreasonably aggressive—in fact been routed game, set and match. Which didn't improve her temper, so that she said incautiously when she should have just shut up if she couldn't concede defeat gracefully, 'Mr Matthews, I've been trying very hard to be *very* nice to you this morning but . . .'

'So I noticed,' he drawled but his eyes laughed at her. 'Sometimes one's better nature gets swamped, though, doesn't it?'

'I . . .'

'I know, because I have the same problem with my better nature sometimes,' he went on gravely but with his eyes still amused. 'Who would have thought we were two of a kind in any respect?'

Nyree put a hand to her head wearily and finally conceded defeat. 'All right, I'm sorry, but can we get on with this?'

'Sure,' he said easily. 'So you're not going to tell me what else was bothering you?'

'No—there was nothing,' she lied and looked him straight in the eyes.

His lips twitched. 'If you say so. Would it help if I carried your pack?'

'No. I'll be fine. Thank you all the same but I'm really as strong as a horse.' The faintly bitter note in her voice was unwitting, and she hoped it was lost on him, but had the feeling it was a hollow hope. Her shoulders slumped—she had certainly made a mess of things this morning, and the worst part of it was, she wasn't sure why she was in such a state. Well, why she was out of control, so to speak. But one thing *was* sure, she would have to improve, because if Reid Matthews ever found out the real reason for her . . . Her lips parted in horror at the mere thought and involuntarily her green gaze flickered to his and for a long, heart-stopping moment they stared into each other's eyes.

But all he said eventually, was, 'Ready?'

'I . . . yes,' she answered huskily.

It took them an hour to reach Leeke's homestead, but for the most part it had been a pleasant walk through the sunlit bush after that steep climb. And Simon, complete with Nyree's binoculars and camera slung around his neck, had particularly enjoyed examining and snapping the fabulous views.

'That was a brainwave,' Reid had said. 'I now know what to get him for Christmas. But is he safe with your camera?'

'It's not a very expensive one, and I've shown him how to use it. He's very careful.'

But Simon expressed his disappointment at the homestead because it was so small.

'Well,' his father said, consulting the guide book, 'only two people lived in it, Ralph and Lizzie Leeke, so it didn't have to be big. And I suppose a lot of the material had to be shipped over from the mainland and carried up here so . . .'

'It seems funny,' Simon broke in, 'to want to live

here all alone. There was no one else on the island then.'

'Some people like that. I suppose Ralph might have fished and it says here Lizzie raised sheep. What do you think, Nyree?'

Nyree looked around. The little wooden homestead dating back to the nineteen twenties was surrounded by a park and through it wandered peacocks, ducks and some magnificent orange and black strutting roosters. Between a fold in the green, bush-clad hills, the waters of the Pacific danced and glittered in the sunlight.

'If you wanted to get away from the madding crowd this would be the place to do it,' she said softly.

'You're not wrong,' Reid agreed wryly. 'Time to have a break and a cup of coffee?' he suggested.

'Oh, definitely,' she agreed ruefully.

So they took off their knapsacks and sat down at a rough-hewn table beneath a shady tree and Reid poured the coffee from a Thermos, while Simon was content with a soft drink and an apple and presently went off to explore.

Nyree sipped the hot, strong, reviving liquid and concentrated her thoughts on the mundane. Such as the fact that Reid Matthews' luggage had arrived mysteriously before the first scheduled flight was due from Rockhampton—and what influence had achieved that, she could only guess at. Then she found herself wondering what he did, how he had made his money, and discovered that nothing he had said gave her any kind of clue. He could be anything, she reflected, yet she couldn't visualise him sitting behind a desk somehow. It would have to be something more active, surely . . .

It was Simon who interrupted her thoughts by calling excitedly from the other side of the homestead, 'Nyree! Come and look at this!'

She bit her lip then said swiftly, 'You go. Tell him I need a rest because I didn't sleep very well last . . .' She broke off and coloured. 'I'm sure he didn't mean to exclude you,' she said lamely.

'I wish I could be so sure but I'll go. Only I think I'll say you . . . want to soak up the atmosphere. That could be just as true too, couldn't it?'

It was strange how the atmosphere got to her. Or perhaps not so strange because she *was* trying desperately not to relive their earlier conversation as she watched Reid stroll out of sight after that parting shot.

And she acknowledged later, as one loner to another pair of loners, Ralph and Lizzie Leeke, the fascination was easy to kindle. But whatever, her thoughts seemed to slip into another channel and it was as if the peace and timelessness of the old homestead slipped beneath her skin and her imagination took wings . . .

So that she could see herself as châtelaine of this home but in an earlier time, an even more pioneering one, so that she was dressed not in the style of the nineteen twenties but earlier, in an era when she would always wear her hair pinned up even on an uninhabited island. When she and her husband—she couldn't quite picture him—made the decision to carve out their own niche in the wilderness and she took all the hardship in her stride, living under canvas while their little house slowly took shape.

She imagined herself ordering books from the mainland so that she could identify the different birds and butterflies and banksias. She could imagine her great delight when a sewing-machine arrived and the pride of place it would probably take in the parlour, next to the small dresser which held a few treasured pieces of china that she had cherished through long voyages and perhaps years of incarceration in packing boxes.

She pictured herself with children clinging to her skirts as she waved her—still faceless—husband off on a fishing trip, and the gun that would be kept loaded on top of the wardrobe because she was frequently alone, and who knew what sort of strangers could land on their island paradise. She pictured the children growing, little girls with long hair and long pinafores helping her with the chores, and boys, more ragged perhaps, helping her with the sheep; she pictured herself teaching them to read and write and simple arithmetic—and the day when her carefully saved money from her wool fleeces would be used to send them to the mainland, to relations perhaps and proper schools.

She could picture it all, except the man. And she pondered what sort of a man it would be who could persuade a wife willingly to give up civilisation for his ideal of independence. Surely there would have to be a fierce bond between them, an enduring passion—a never-failing sense of delight between them in those most private moments when she unpinned her hair, revealed what only he had ever seen, and accepted his love . . .

'A penny for them,' a voice said beside her and she came back to reality with a jolt.

'Oh! Nothing really, just daydreaming,' she said to Reid Matthews. 'What did Simon have to show you?'

'One of the peacocks obligingly fanned out his tail, but we have it on camera at least three times . . .'

'Nyree!' Simon ran up to her full of what she had missed, with a peacock feather he had found for her. Then he said, quite unselfconsciously, 'Dad reckons the old sheep shed and pen might be interesting to look at. Shall we go that way? The map says they're down there.'

They went that way, although Nyree looked back once or twice, still faintly in the grip of her curious daydream.

The little old shed and yards were barely more than a skeleton of wooden posts but were in the process of being restored. They were at the head of the inlet known as Leeke's Creek, not far from the homestead, where a boat could land at high tide. And with Simon as navigator, they proceeded the short distance to Leeke's Beach, a long golden curve of sand that stretched to Putney Point, and there was not a soul visible on it as they broke through the bush, although there were a couple of yachts moored offshore.

Reid raised his eyebrows and whistled. 'Some beach.'

'It's beautiful, isn't it,' Nyree agreed. 'That's one of the fascinations of Keppel, such marvellous beaches and so many of them—much better beaches than the Whitsundays, I think.'

'Oh? You know the Whitsundays?'

'Yes. Well. And they're fabulous, but when the tide goes out up there you're often left with a rather unattractive mudflat. Here, all the bottoms are sandy, but of course the coral isn't so spectacular. It's getting close to lunch time. Should we walk up to Putney Point or have it here?'

He shrugged and consulted Simon who decided in favour of Putney Point. In fact he scampered off ahead of them, still full of enthusiasm and energy.

'It ... it could be working,' Nyree said a little wonderingly.

'It's certainly relieved some of the tension,' Reid said but non-committally, so that she looked at him with a query in her eyes.

He shrugged. 'There've been times before when I've thought I was getting through to him only to have him clam up again.'

'Does Simon ever talk about his mother?'

'No. Never.'

'I think you've got to talk about her,' Nyree said urgently. 'It might be awfully hard for you, but ...'

'Do you think I haven't tried?' he cut in. 'Do you ... can you imagine what it's like to have a curtain come down in his eyes while he looks at you? Nothing else changes, he doesn't rant or rave or even look particularly sad, he just cuts himself off totally.'

'He probably ...' Nyree hesitated. 'He must know you rejected each other, you and his mother, but that she ... cared for him. He must have her memory very close in his heart and be afraid of compromising it.'

'Yes,' Reid said flatly.

She looked at him. 'Does he understand that you didn't know?'

He turned a suddenly harsh blue gaze on her. 'I don't know what he *understands*, but he does know the facts ... Do you mind if we leave it for a while?'

'Yes, I do mind,' she said slowly. 'I'm ... very fond of Simon. I ...' she gestured as if to qualify this statement, 'he reminds me of myself a bit, but also I can't deny that he ... tugged at my heartstrings almost immediately. He—he's a darling,' she said a little hoarsely and added almost fiercely, 'so don't try to freeze me out now. I'm in this for better or worse. *You* wanted me in!'

The hard glint left Reid's eyes as he studied her tilted jaw and frustrated expression. 'Are we—fighting again?' he queried with a smile growing in his eyes.

'You are ... this time it's your fault!' she said indignantly.

'So it is,' he conceded and reached for her hand. 'Sorry. At times it's hard not to get depressed and wary. How do you feel about another swim?'

'I ...' She looked at her hand in his. 'It might be what I need.'

They ate their picnic lunches after swimming—small feasts of cold ham and chicken, salad and fruit. Then Simon wandered off to explore the rocks, and Nyree cleared up and poured the last two cups of coffee from the Thermos, handed Reid his and sat down on her towel.

Her costume was a soft jade-green lycra one-piece and showed off the golden tan she had acquired, not to mention her figure. She wasn't thinking of it, however, as she sipped her coffee. She was thinking instead that Reid had been right, she had started out this day feeling taut and aching—mentally, more than physically—whereas now she was feeling more relaxed, much more. Although she would probably sleep like a dog tonight ...

'What were you daydreaming about back at Leeke's cottage, Nyree?' Reid said into the silence.

She turned to see that he was stretched out on his towel with his head propped on one hand.

'I was imagining what it would be like to be a pioneer,' she said wryly.

'I think you might have made a good pioneer,' he said slowly.

'I don't know ... but there *was* something— appealing about my daydreams, I guess. Something about a life that was sort of—back to the basics, kind of thing. In reality, though, six weeks of it would probably be enough to send you round the bend.'

'Some people still prefer it.'

'Yes, I know. There's a family that lives on the next beach, Svendsen's Beach, and although I suppose they have more mod cons than the Leekes had it has to be a very different kind of life. The beach is named after them—oh, I think it's a sort of island mania that gets to you when you come to these places.'

'I know what you mean,' he said unexpectedly. Then, 'Tell me about yourself, Nyree.'

She hesitated then rolled over to lie on her front with her chin supported in her hands. 'You mean a potted life history? Well, my mother died when I was two and my father was a ship's captain, so I didn't see an awful lot of him while I was growing up, but what time we did spend together was great. He was madly into boats of all types, and although you would imagine that in his holidays he'd want to get away from the sea, he didn't. We had—I still have it—a twenty-five-foot yacht, that he used to keep up at Shute Harbour, and every holiday we had, we used to go up there and live on it. In fact one year, when I was about fourteen, he took long leave, a year, and we lived up there, cruising Whitsundays and further north for all that time.'

'What about school?'

'I did it by correspondence and he helped me. He was very hot on education, but not only on the conventional kind. He taught me all he knew about navigation, for example, and sailing. Then the next year I went on a round-the-world cruise with him—on his liner, that is—and got a crash course in three months, on the world. In fact I think one way or the other, he taught me more than I learnt elsewhere.'

'He's dead now, too?'

'Yes. Six years ago.'

'And who looked after you in between times?'

Her lips twitched. 'My aunt—my mother's sister. She's still alive but she's as eccentric as they come.' She released her chin and scooped up a handful of sand which she let trickle through her long slender fingers.

'In what way?' he asked with an intrigued look.

'Well, she thoroughly disapproved of my father taking me off the way he did, as much as she disapproved of anything that didn't have to do with animals and plants and the environment. She's a naturalist, and she just can't see the point of boats. Between the two of them I sometimes used to wonder if I'd grow up with a mania of some kind, but my father assured me I took after my mother, who was just a normal womanly woman. But in between campaigning against the devastation of rain-forests or sandmining on beaches, or flitting off to Tasmania to verify a sighting of the Tasmanian tiger which she was sure—still is—still exists although the last verified sighting was years and years ago, she found time to give me a home and look upon me as the daughter she never had.'

'Well, it's no wonder,' Reid said with a grin.

'What?'

'That you strike me as an . . . unconventional sort of person. You must admit it wasn't a very conventional childhood. But then you chose a very conventional career. I would have expected something different.'

Nyree was silent for a time, scooping more sand. 'I think I went through a stage in my late teens when I just wanted to lead a life like the girl next door. That might have been why I chose teaching. But I haven't regretted it.'

'And this?' He waved a hand in the direction of Simon who could be heard whistling happily away as he pottered about the rocks.

She explained.

'It must cut into your social life.'

'I don't have a particularly social life,' she said quietly.

'Does that mean there are no men in your life?' he asked idly.

Nyree's fingers stilled and she watched some grains

of sand slip on to the little pile beneath. She raised her green eyes to his. 'Yes,' she said abruptly. Then she jumped up in one long lithe movement adding, 'If we go now, we can get around Putney Point, over the rocks. If we leave it much longer the tide will be too high and we'll have to climb over the hill. I think we should go now.'

'I'm sorry,' he said from behind her as she pulled on her T-shirt, 'I didn't mean to trespass.'

'You weren't,' she replied briefly and untruthfully as she reached for her shorts.

'Then I would have to guess that someone once hurt you rather badly, Nyree,' he said.

She straightened, buttoning the waistband, and she ran her fingers through her hair which was all but dry, and with deft, practised movements plaited it and pulled a rubber band out of the pocket of her shorts to secure it. 'Yes,' she said at last, 'you're a good guesser.'

'Only average,' he murmured. 'You did mention last night that you despised men.'

She grimaced. 'Did I say that? I must have been very . . . annoyed.'

'You were. Want to tell me about it?'

Nyree took a breath. 'No. No,' she said confusedly. 'All I want to do is *forget* about it. And I want to get around those rocks before the tide comes in so . . .'

'All right,' he said easily and as if he were placating Simon. 'Subject closed. Any plans for when we get back?'

With an effort Nyree tried to think, but it was Simon who supplied the answer. He came running up to say excitedly, 'They're para-sailing off the spit. Can we go and watch?'

'Why not. Ever tried it, Nyree?'

Simon answered for her again. 'No. And she won't. She says the one thing she draws the line at is anything to do with parachutes, although I've told her it's got to be quite safe. I'd do it but I'm not old enough—you have to be fourteen.'

The possibility this raised must have occurred to Reid and Nyree at the same time because as she looked at him quickly he murmured, 'How fortunate I have nothing against parachutes—yet.'

'I'm sure it is very safe . . .'

'Dad? Are you going to try it? '

'I think I might give it a go, Simon. Then I'll be able to report back to you, won't I?'

'Oh, boy! Let's go!'

Reid and Nyree laughed quietly together as he grabbed his knapsack, adjusted the binoculars and camera and bounded off.

'It never occurred to me to win his approval this way,' Reid said wryly. 'Any more gladiatorial sports I could try my hand at?'

'Well, there's archery . . .'

'No. Never held a bow and arrow in my life.'

'Uh . . . tennis? I'd be quite happy if you were to beat me in a game of tennis some time.'

'Done!' He grinned down at her, standing in front of her in only his blue shorts and with his hands on his hips.

Nyree grinned back, then she blinked as the oddest thing happened to her. She found herself thinking that here was a man who could fill her faceless image of . . . *no*, she corrected herself with an unnatural skip to her heartbeat. No. All that they had in common was the fact that, physically, he was a match for her, if not more than a match; that was all and that certainly wasn't enough.

She blinked again and hoped she was only imagining the slight feeling of heat in her cheeks, because the thought was really outrageous. She turned away.

CHAPTER THREE

REFLECTIONS of the previous day filtered through Nyree's mind as she woke slowly the next morning.

Reflections of Simon for example, thawing slightly towards his father and even taking pride in him. That had come about because of the para-sailing. When it had been Reid's turn to go up, the breeze had become capricious—dying right down, in fact, once he was aloft, so that it had been difficult to bring him in.

Nyree had begun to feel anxious herself as the boat had made several false runs parallel to the beach for the descent. And she and Simon had stood hand in hand on the beach, shading their eyes from the sun.

'They'll have to put him down in the water,' Simon had said knowledgeably. 'I just hope . . .'

But the next run had been successful and Reid had landed on his feet like a feather, and he'd been laughing and exhilarated and obviously quite fearless. And to help matters along, the small crowd gathered on the spit to watch the afternoon para-sailing, including Dean among them, had applauded. That was when Simon had looked fleetingly proud.

It was later, Nyree remembered, that she had noticed Simon watching her and his father curiously a couple of times. As if assessing their relationship or at least finding it food for thought. How strange, she had thought, that my approval might help—only to

55

remember then that she didn't particularly approve of Reid Matthews.

But, she thought, still lying in bed the next morning watching the sunlight creeping into the room, for a day that began so uncertainly, it ended rather peacefully. With me reading Simon a bedtime story and Reid reading his newspaper quite as if we were a . . . family.

She grimaced and sat up at last, cautiously though, as if testing herself, wondering if the way she had felt the previous morning was going to slide over her. After all, she was still alone in the same sense. But all she could detect was a feeling of well-being because the sun was shining, she was really rested . . . and she had a definable objective ahead of her. Ah! she mused with a wry little smile. So that's it! You feel needed again and on much surer ground, at least . . . well, definitely with Simon.

But she sobered as she wondered if it was that simple. Can I hide behind other peple's children for ever? The thought crossed her mind from nowhere . . . Is that what I do? *If* I do, is it . . . wrong?

Her green eyes clouded briefly with confusion, but just at that moment Simon knocked on the interconnecting door and called through that he and Reid were going for a sprint up the beach before breakfast and did she want to come?

'Definitely,' she called back.

Two days passed in increasing amiability, as Nyree thought of it. They swam, they sailed, they explored the island, Nyree and Simon showing Reid special places they had already visited, but whereas they had tramped through the bush to get to different beaches Reid, much to Simon's delight, hired one of the sleek little speedboats to take them. Not having to walk meant he could introduce his son to the delights of fishing, and they had water-skiing lessons—another area outside Nyree's ken that Reid proved himself to be proficient at. And they generally tired themselves out so thoroughly, at least she and Simon did—she got the feeling Reid could go on for ever—it was a pleasure to fall into bed not long after dinner.

It also, this intense activity, provided the frame of mind to be calm and friendly, Nyree noted. None of the tensions that had exploded between them almost on impact—the thought caused her to smile a little wryly—surfaced. So that when Simon said to her out of the blue, 'You like my Dad, don't you, Nyree?' she had been able to answer serenely, 'Yes I do, Simon,' and only then stop to consider with a curious little tremor how surprisingly true this was. But he's not always like this, she reminded herself a moment later. Neither am I. It's really an act for Simon's benefit, this . . .

Yet she couldn't quite shake off the feeling that it was all too natural for an act . . . And she found herself watching Reid Matthews covertly for a while and with a sudden feeling of confusion—one that she resolutely banished, without even trying to analyse it. Just go on as you have been, Nyree, she cautioned herself. Don't spoil things.

But on his fourth full day with them, things changed of their own accord. It began with a game of tennis in the afternoon. Simon came along to watch them and Nyree murmured to Reid, 'This is another occasion where I give you the opportunity to shine in your son's eyes, isn't it?' But she said it with humour.

'I . . .' He studied her narrowly for a moment, then, 'Why do I get the feeling this could be a hollow victory?'

'I'm also a tennis coach as well as an English teacher,' she said demurely.

'Is that so!' His lips twisted ruefully. 'Then let's make a proper game of this.'

'I wouldn't dream of it . . . well, I've had my moment of ego,' she confessed wryly. 'Otherwise I wouldn't have mentioned it, would I?'

'At least you're honest,' he commented with a grin.

'Sometimes . . .' she was surprised to hear herself say and then because she couldn't—didn't want to—tangle with the veils of her mind, she turned away rather abruptly and strode on to the court.

But as they were warming up, Dean arrived and Simon decided it would be far more interesting to spend the afternoon on the beach with him. Reid gave his consent and turned back to Nyree with his eyebrows raised and a smile playing on his lips.

She said nothing but she thought, why not? Although I'll probably regret it. I'm sure he plays tennis as well as he does everything else.

He did but she didn't regret it. She played the first set with inspiration, agility and a cunning serve and she won it, although she had some luck. He was having trouble with his serve but he got it going in the second set and won six-three. But the third set was the thriller. Nyree thought at first he was having trouble with his serve again, then realised he was toning it down deliberately, which annoyed her at first until she admitted to herself that it was ridiculous to imagine she could beat a man with a slamming, hundred-mile-an-hour serve, and that this way at least they could meet on more equal ground. So she wiped all annoyance from her mind and settled down to play the set of her life.

He won but the score was seven games to five which satisfied Nyree. She said as they shook hands over the net, 'Thanks for the handicap.'

'What handicap?'

'Your serve. At full strength it would have ended this contest much sooner.'

'I was hoping you wouldn't notice—and you were right, you're pretty good. Could I buy you a long, long cool drink?'

'I was hoping you'd say that . . .'

Simon was still playing happily on the beach and they took their drinks, by a curious coincidence, Nyree thought, to the same table she had sat at the day Reid had arrived.

It was also curious how much better she felt than on that day. Tired, yes, and she could feel a trickle of sweat between her breasts and knew her shirt was clinging to her damply, but pleasantly run out of energy, relaxed and at peace with the world . . . well, at peace with him, she thought slowly. Reid Matthews, who . . .

'Oh, there you are!' a voice said from behind, and

she turned to see a comfortably plump, pinkly sunburnt woman approaching. 'How do you do?' she went on. 'I'm Jean Porter, Dean's mother, and you must be Simon's parents—Mr and Mrs Matthews, isn't it? How do you do?' she said again, extending a hand to Reid who had risen.

'Uh . . . how do you do?' Reid said. 'I . . .'

But Jean Porter swept on, oblivious of the gaffe she'd made, 'I've come to ask if you'll lend us Simon this evening,' she said earnestly. 'My husband and I have decided to take our kids round to Putney Beach for a barbecue tonight. We've spoken to the cook and he's provided us with the food, and Les, that's my husband, is going to show off his boy-scouting skills. But the thing is, Dean informs me his life will be quite blighted if Simon doesn't come as well. We'd deliver him back to your door and we'd take great care of him, Mrs Matthews,' she said to Nyree.

For the life of her Nyree couldn't help colouring and feeling supremely awkward and helpless until Reid came to her rescue.

'I'm afraid there's been a . . . probably perfectly natural misunderstanding, Mrs Porter . . .'

'Oh do call me Jean! There has? You don't want your son to come . . .'

'No, no,' Reid said hastily. 'It's just that he's not—our son.'

'Not . . .?' Jean Porter's forehead creased.

'I'm not his mother.' Nyree found her voice at last. 'And I'm not . . . Mrs Matthews. I'm a paid companion. Uh . . . Mr Matthews thought he mightn't be able to get away for this holiday so . . . he hired me.'

'Well! Well,' Jean Porter said bewilderedly, 'now I come to think of it, Simon does call you . . . Nyree, is it? Yes, but I just thought—some children do and he never said—oh dear, I just *assumed*. Do forgive me,' she said, worried.

'Of course.' Reid smiled at her and pulled out a chair for her. 'Won't you join us?'

'Thank you,' she replied, obviously charmed, and bursting with curiosity now. 'Just for a minute—so poor little Simon has no mother—oh, there I go just assuming things again!'

'No, he doesn't,' Reid murmured.

'Then,' Jean Porter turned to Nyree, 'for someone hired, you've done a marvellous job with him. He's so natural with you—in fact the three of you seem so natural together now—quite like a family! Oh dear, I must run, I have our youngest down on the beach— but you'll let Simon come with us tonight, won't you?'

'Certainly,' said Simon's father. 'I'm sure I would be blighting *Simon's* life if I said no! Thank you very much—Jean.'

'It's a pleasure! Now, what I thought would be wise would be to take them back to their rooms so they can relax for a while, then bundle them up in warm clothing and we'll leave just before sunset . . .'

Her going seemed to create a vacuum until Nyree looked up and across at Reid to find him watching her. And for a moment their eyes locked in a gaze she didn't seem able to break, but didn't understand either.

This time it was Simon who rescued her by arriving at the table in a state of high excitement about the proposed barbecue.

'I think Jean might be right,' Reid said wryly, 'about relaxing them for a while. Otherwise they'll be exhausted before they begin. What say you, young Simon? Should we go back to the room and be quiet for a while?' He ruffled Simon's fair hair casually, something he wouldn't have done two days ago— something Simon wouldn't have accepted but now he laughingly acquiesced.

But on their way back they encountered Amy Kelly with a mixed group of people, and Reid stopped to chat while Simon and Nyree went on ahead, Nyree thinking that she was surprised they hadn't bumped into Amy Kelly sooner.

It was Simon's parting shot just before he left to join Dean's family on the beach that caused Reid some amusement.

Simon said, 'It's worked out well, hasn't it? Nyree won't be lonely because she'll have you to keep her company. See you later!'

'Do you get the feeling there's a reversal of roles here?' Reid asked wryly, as they waved the party off from Nyree's veranda.

She hesitated then said, 'He's very sweet.'

'And we have an evening ahead of us . . .'

'Oh, look,' Nyree interrupted, 'I think I might make it an early night. You go ahead and . . .' She stopped.

'What makes you think I don't intend to make it a

fairly early night?' he countered.

Nyree tried to think and finally said lightly, 'You deserve a break from early nights. I'm sure they're more a penance to you than they have been to me. Why don't you ... I'm sure Miss Kelly would be happy if you joined her—them. I could wait up for Simon and put him to bed so you wouldn't ...'

'We could both join Miss Kelly until ten,' he said idly.

Nyree took a breath. They had moved back into her room and were both still in their tennis gear although she'd added a tracksuit top.

'That's not something you'd care to do?' he queried.

'No,' she said steadily.

'You—think they'd make you feel unwelcome because you're a glorified nanny?'

Nyree started to say that Amy had already done that but she bit her lip and shrugged and said instead, 'You don't have to worry about being "social" with me.'

'I thought we'd been fairly social for the last couple of days.'

'Well, that's different. Look ...'

But he broke in. 'Are you afraid of being social—as you call it—with me without Simon to chaperon us then?'

A glint of anger lit Nyree's green eyes. 'I'm not afraid of anything at all to do with you!' she retorted. 'I just don't enjoy the kind of things Miss Kelly enjoys. I'm not into discoing and ... that kind of thing and ...'

'Neither am I ...'

But she swept on, '. . . and I'd stick out like a . . . what did you say?'

He grinned a little wickedly. 'I said, neither am I.'

'So why . . .'

'You brought *Miss* Kelly up in the first place,' he said gravely and added, 'By the way her name is Amy. But I've been trying to avoid her for the last couple of days because not only do I not go in for the kind of entertainment she enjoys, I also don't go in for being as blatantly pursued—as that.'

Nyree shut her mouth with a click. 'I . . . you could have fooled me, then,' she said with a touch of grimness. 'You gave . . . on the night you arrived, you gave the impression you were lapping it up.'

'Did I?' he said softly.

'*Yes*, and don't try to deny . . .' Nyree broke off and shut her mouth firmly again, but again the simmering resentment she felt would not be contained. 'If you feel that way about Amy Kelly,' she said deliberately, 'why did you . . . trap me into sounding such a snob in reverse? And why—I mean, you *did* give that impression . . . you know you did! That's not very fair to her, surely?'

He shrugged and had the grace to look fleetingly rueful. 'I've been fielding Amy for some time now—I know her father rather well and . . . perhaps I've thought it kinder . . . but you're right, perhaps it wasn't. That night, though, you . . . looked down at her from some Olympian height with such utter, cool superiority, I couldn't resist taking a tilt at you, I'm afraid.'

'But . . . all right,' Nyree said stiffly, her cheeks

reddening, 'I apologise for offending your friends whom you don't even like anyway, but . . .'

'Oh, you don't have to apologise,' he said, his blue eyes glinting with laughter. 'I should be the one to apologise, which I do.'

Nyree's eyes positively flashed with anger at having the ground cut away from her in this manner—being left with nothing to say when she wanted to say a whole host of things about men in general and Reid Matthews in particular. But, however galling and angering it was, she was learning some wisdom, and this time she did shut her mouth firmly.

But he took ruthless advantage of her silence by saying with sudden seriousness, 'Honestly, Nyree, if we both have the same intentions tonight—and after experiencing your prowess on a tennis court the last thing I feel like is a late night—isn't it a bit ridiculous to eat separately? Is that what you have in mind? In the same dining-room? All *I* had in mind was having dinner together and then perhaps a nightcap while we wait for Simon.'

She stared at him speechlessly for a moment, then helplessly for a moment or two more.

Until he put out a hand and took one of hers. And said, 'Please. I'll try to make amends.'

She transferred her gaze down to her hand in his and thought, strangely, of their tennis match—so evenly matched but only when he'd wanted it to be— and an inward tremor ran down her spine; and for a moment she wished fervently that she could say no. But it would be ridiculous . . .

'All right. Provided you don't mind me taking at least an hour to get ready. I . . . I'm suffering from *your* prowess on a tennis court.'

He released her hand and stepped back. 'Take as long as you like.' And their eyes clashed again.

Nyree was the first to look away.

She took fifty-five minutes to get ready. She didn't stay in the shower for half an hour, but she did wash her hair and had to blow dry it, and while she did that, she wondered what to wear. Then it occurred to her that any indecision about her clothes would invest the coming evening with the aura of a 'date', which was the last thing it could be. So, as soon as her hair was dry, she walked over to the built-in wardrobe and unhooked the first oufit that came to hand.

This turned out to be a pale grey denim skirt that fitted her hips smoothly then flared to mid-calf length. With it she usually teamed a hyacinth-pink blouse that she wore over the skirt and belted just below her waist. The belt was leather but soft and supple and two-toned, bronze and a dusky pink and it looped through two beaten silver rings. She had a choice of shoes to go with the outfit, a pair of bronze-brown flatties or an exquisite, so she thought, pair of pale grey kid court shoes cut low over her high arch but with higher heels than she usually wore.

She grimaced faintly at her random choice, because despite the denim and the overblouse, on her the outfit looked quite formal and elegant—more than she wanted to look tonight, anyway . . .

But then she accused herself of splitting hairs and

got dressed resolutely. And with five minutes to go she eyed the interconnecting door then turned away, looked down at her feet and after the barest hesitation slipped off the bronze flatties and slipped them into the pale grey, high-heeled kid shoes.

For a moment the unaccustomed height made her feel insecure then, as she stood tall and proudly upright, she felt—it was hard to say—as if the outfit was properly finished, as if the flat shoes had been a sop to a society of pygmies.

A faint grin curved her lips at her absurd flight of fancy and she bent her head and was observing her narrow feet so beautifully shod when, with just a light triple knock, Reid Matthews opened the door between their rooms.

She lifted her head and felt a rush of colour come to her cheeks and, unbelievably she raised her hands to her warm cheeks like a little girl caught being vain, then took refuge in tucking her hair, which was billowing with life and vitality, back smoothly.

He looked down at her feet, looked up and raised an eyebrow because she was about three inches taller and their eyes were almost on a level.

'New?' he asked.

'The shoes? Yes. How did you know?'

'They look brand new,' he said with a glimmer of amusement in his blue eyes. 'And you were gazing down at them so admiringly.'

She smiled ruefully and turned away to pick up a silvery-grey fluffy mohair jacket.

'You're also taller,' he observed.

'I know. That's why I don't normally wear heels

this high. I tend to feel like a giraffe.' She turned back and he was standing right behind her. He was wearing a pair of fawn trousers, a cream shirt open at the neck and a brown corduroy sports jacket. His dark hair was neatly brushed, and for the first time she noticed a few silver threads in it.

'But not with me,' he said quietly.

She half smiled but didn't reply.

Captain Cook discovered the Keppel group of islands in May, 1770 and, as he did quite frequently on his voyage up the east coast of Australia, named them after naval personages of the day. Augustus Keppel was a Rear Admiral at the time, but by 1782 he was appointed First Lord of the Admiralty—a fitting fate for a boy wonder. He had joined the navy at the age of ten and by the age of nineteen had his first command.

He was still honoured on the island by having the restaurant not only named after him but bearing a distinctly nautical favour. At one end there was a print of his portrait by Reynolds, although Captain Cook was not forgotten—there was also a portrait of him and copies of his log books on display. And one could be forgiven for imagining one was dining in the large saloon of a tall old ship, for the walls were wood-panelled, there was a display of semaphore flags and helm, and, a touch that had vastly intrigued Simon, the lights suspended from the ceiling not only looked like old-fashioned flame ones but they swung backwards and forwards slowly as if one were indeed on the high seas.

And at night the atmosphere was dim and intimate.

Reid gave their room numbers and, when asked whether they would like to join a larger table, he declined.

Nyree glanced around briefly as they were taken to a table for two in a quiet corner, but she couldn't make out Amy Kelly, nor were they hailed, to her distinct relief, and it occurred to her that she was feeling oddly tense.

Their waitress came swiftly to take their orders and hard on her heels came the wine steward.

Reid looked at her enquiringly. 'Do you think we deserve a bottle of wine?'

'Why not?' she murmured.

'Any preference?'

She shook her head and he consulted the list and ordered them a Richmond Grove Chardonnay. A girl was playing the piano on the small stage and singing softly.

The wine came but Nyree couldn't think of a thing to say, nor did Reid seem eager to make conversation, but then he didn't seem to be uncomfortable either, which she was—as if her usual poise had deserted her, or as if the hand of fate was just beginning to make its presence felt. Something was there below the surface of her mind, she reflected. Don't tell me I'm about to sink into a slough of despond again . . . no, I won't let it happen.

'You know, I hardly know anything about you,' she said, speaking the first words that came to mind, and realising that, while it might be a conversational ploy, it was also true.

'What would you like to know?'

She shrugged. 'Where you come from, what you do—that kind of thing.'

He considered. 'I was born not far from here as a matter of fact. On a cattle station west of Rockhampton. My father was station manager, my mother, station book-keeper.'

Nyree looked surprised.

'Yes, it was rather unusual,' he agreed. 'She had a powerful mind and personality, my mother. She ran the family as she ran the books, thoroughly uncompromisingly. My father used to enjoy going away mustering as often as he could get away with it. So did I.' He grinned suddenly. 'My poor sister was left to bear the brunt of our beloved mother. Still, I shouldn't complain. She saved enough to put me through university, although I paid her back every penny, and I'm sure she always had our best interests at heart— why are you looking at me like that?' he enquired.

Nyree blinked, then their soup was served so she was saved from having to reply immediately. And she eventually said, 'No reason. How was I looking at you?'

Reid stared at her thoughtfully with his soup spoon half-way to his mouth, but she preserved an innocent expression. But it had become clear to her, although she didn't see any necessity to share it with him, where his particular antipathy towards overbearing women came from.

'I don't know,' he said wryly, and drank his soup in silence for a time.

'What did you study?'

'Veterinary Science . . .'

This time Nyree made no effort to hide her surprise.

'That obviously amazes you,' he said.

'Yes, but I don't know why, really. Well, . . .' She stopped. You're very wealthy, according to Gwen, she had been going to say. Although it wasn't impossible to be a rich vet, she was sure, but . . .

She shook her head ruefully. 'I don't know why.'

'I'm not precisely a practising vet these days,' he said. 'At university I met up with a chemistry student who was interested in animals, and eventually we went into business together manufacturing products mainly for cattle, sheep and horses. Dips, drenches—parasite control products and things like that.'

'Oh!' Nyree looked at him with new interest and respect. 'And it's been a successful venture?'

'It was a long, hard slog at first, but we've come into our own, more or less. Our products are in use all over Australia, and we recently had a breakthrough in New Zealand.'

'And what do you do exactly?' Their pepper steaks had arrived.

'What do I do?' He cut into his steak. 'I spend a lot of time travelling around outback cattle and sheep stations advising them how to use the products for optimum performance, keeping tabs on control programmes, observing the effectiveness of our products . . . that kind of thing.'

Nyree ate in silence for a time thinking, well, that explains the tan and possibly why Simon is at boarding-school. 'I'm sure your mother must be proud of you,' she said at last. 'And your sister?'

'Oh, she survived my mother as well,' he said a shade drily. 'She married the chemist, so it's very much a family business. Amanda, as it turned out, inherited mother's drive and initiative in the form of a formidable instinct for marketing.'

'So your home base is in Brisbane?'

'Yes. I live with Amanda and Harold in a self-contained flat—if I want it to be, although that's a fairly recent development. Which brings us to Simon.' He pushed his plate away and glanced at her rather sharply, she thought.

'We don't have to go into that,' she said tranquilly, and reached for her wine.

'Aren't you the least bit curious?' he queried with a mocking glint back in his eyes.

Nyree twirled her glass and watched the golden liquid catch the light. 'I know the facts. You don't have to tell me any more . . .' As soon as she said it, though, Nyree realised she was curious and that it had been lurking in a corner of her mind like a question mark—what kind of a woman had Simon's mother been? Reid's wife . . . beautiful? Yes, undoubtedly that. Had he loved her and lost her—but how? Well, he can be . . . hard, she reminded herself.

'And what,' Reid said into the silence, 'if I wanted to tell you?'

'I . . .' Nyree stopped and wondered why she felt as if some dark wings had brushed her mind. 'All right,' she said reluctantly.

'It doesn't matter,' he returned brusquely, and looked away.

Nyree bit her lip as she studied the harsh

unhappiness of his expression. 'I think . . . I think you had better tell me,' she said softly.

'It's not a very pleasant story,' he said roughly, 'as you rightly surmised, no doubt.'

'Then it might help to tell me,' she said levelly. 'Sometimes it does help to share things with a stranger, someone impartial.'

His lips twisted. 'Are we strangers?'

'Virtually. And I am capable of being impartial.'

'I believe you,' he said slowly. 'Well, here goes—I divorced Simon's mother when she told me she was pregnant by another man. I provided her with her fare to go home—she was English, so was the lover— and the whole thing was handled by lawyers from there on. I made her quite a large settlement so that I could wash my hands of her. I never for one minute considered the child was my own—she *told* me it wasn't. She told me it was due two months later than it was actually born, which put the time of conception after we'd stopped sleeping with each other . . . I know now that Simon was a perfectly normal, full-term baby. I told you it wasn't pleasant,' he said to the look in Nyree's eyes.

'But . . .' She looked at him in a bewildered way. 'Go on.'

'I mean,' she said helplessly, 'what happened to make things go . . . go so terribly wrong? Did you never love each other?'

'If we did,' he said impassively, 'it was a fairly temporary state of affairs. It certainly didn't stand up to my expectations of what a wife should be, nor her expectations of marriage. I don't suppose it makes much sense to you, but . . .'

'Oh, it does,' she said quietly. 'At least in essence—I was just shocked that she should want to deny your own child to you. It seems . . . pretty extreme. But I'm sure no two people can fall out more bitterly than lovers whose expectations clash. Was she a madly liberated kind of woman?'

He was silent, studying her with a faint frown in his eyes. Then he seemed to come back from another place and he nodded. 'Also beautiful, intelligent, spirited, but . . . I don't know how to explain it . . . intent on preserving her freedom at all costs. But in a marriage how can you be free? And it wasn't as if I planned to keep her barefoot and pregnant and tied to the kitchen sink, although,' his lips twisted, 'in all honesty I have to admit I have a tendency to want to be boss. To say,' he murmured drily, 'that I inherited anything from my dear mother doesn't come easily but there you are. Also, I suspect I'm a fairly normal male who hasn't quite adjusted to the new order of things. I mean, even my mother washed and ironed and cooked and maintained a comfortable home—and positively gloried in being a wife and mother. It was her great role in life—it was just that she did it so well, so efficiently, she nearly drove us all mad in the process. Whereas Sylvia,' he paused, 'treated marriage as a convenient love-nest, that's all. I suppose I'm spouting some mixed-up male chauvinist sentiment,' he said with a wry little smile, then sobered, 'but I could have put up with all the rest if I'd felt she was really . . . committed to me. Yet almost from the time she got my ring on her finger she seemed to be trying to tell me and show me she was only committed to herself. And that ... well, let's just say, it brought out the worst in me. I probably don't have to tell you about that.' He pushed his empty wineglass away abruptly.

Nyree's lips trembled into a smile. 'At least you're honest. So it was a fiasco?'

'Yes.'

'And you—and she—probably underestimated her need for freedom. Some people, men and women, are like that and have been down the ages.'

'I think you're right,' he said sombrely. 'I didn't until I found out about Simon, but then I began to understand. Not that I can forgive her, whatever her needs were.'

Nyree waited until their coffee was poured then she said, 'How did you find out?'

'Eighteen months ago she was killed in a car accident. Her parents had looked after Simon more or less since he was born. But they were both elderly and I think to an extent as bewildered by their daughter as I was. They decided the time had come to let me know.'

'She'd told them? Was there ever another man?'

'Not seriously, no. There were other men but nothing permanent. She told them about me and swore them to secrecy. She told them she'd wanted to experience motherhood, but on her own terms. She told them I would never have let a child of mine slip through my fingers and that this was the best way for the child. But at first I didn't believe it. Then I had to go and have a look for myself. There was no doubt.'

'None?'

'No. If you could have taken a composite photo of Amanda and myself at that age, you would have Simon.'

'What about his mother?'

'Facially there's hardly any resemblance at all, but he has her hair and her feet and her walk. I didn't just accept it on face value, though. I verified the date of birth, I even tracked down the doctor who delivered him, I had blood tests taken.' He sighed. 'Then Sylvia's father died while all this was going on and in the space of a few short weeks, her mother just lost touch with reality. She was just . . . lost without him, she was still grieving for Sylvia—they might not have understood her but she was their only child—and she was weakened and muddled by the whole mess, I guess. She died two months later. I brought Simon home and moved in with Harold and Amanda because Amanda was really concerned for Simon and she thought she could be there for him when I couldn't. I suppose,' he hesitated, 'not that I ever thought it would be *easy*, but perhaps I underestimated the damage and the trauma it had all caused Simon. I'd certainly underestimated the devotion and loyalty and *love* he felt for a mother who left him to spend most of his life with his grandparents while she was off doing her own thing,' he said bitterly.

'Children are like that,' Nyree said softly. 'She was probably like a shining star in his life, not often glimpsed but all the more radiant. You . . . loved her once, don't forget.'

He was silent.

'How come he's at boarding-school?' Nyree asked after a time.

'It was his own choice. He asked me about Australian boarding-schools.'

Nyree made a surprised little sound and Reid added, 'He had been a weekly boarder in England for a year. Anyway I discussed it with Amanda and she pointed out—they have no kids yet—that it might help him to be more in the company of boys his own age so I made some enquiries and picked out a suitable school and told them the whole sad story. The headmaster said that Simon would possibly feel less pressured among strangers. That it would be a relief to him not to have to continually cope with a father sprung on him out of the blue when he could still remember his mother and grandparents and what had to be an era of unusual tragedy in his young life. So, with Simon's consent, we agreed to give it a trial run. Simon was quite happy about it,' he said bleakly.

'Oh, Reid,' Nyree said gently, 'it's all perfectly natural—in fact it's a miracle he's not *more* disturbed. But I'm sure with time and care it will come right—I mean, already he's much more natural with you.'

'Thanks to you, Nyree, I don't think he hates me as much but . . .'

'Why Reid!' A familiar purring voice interrupted them and they both looked up to see that Amy Kelly had stopped at the table. 'There you are! Darling, this is Peter Smith,' she introduced.

Reid stood up and shook hands with the man Amy had in tow. 'And this is Nyree Westbrook,' he said in turn.

But Amy contrived to brush Nyree aside. 'Reid, won't you join us? I see you've finished dinner and we have the makings of a really interesting party tonight!'

Nyree blinked and couldn't for a moment believe that the other girl could be so blatant. Not that she knew Peter Smith's circumstances, but he was looking down at Amy with unmistakable interest, while Amy had glanced provocatively from Reid to him and back, a look that said as clearly as if she'd spoken to Reid ... I'm available but there is competition ...

'Thanks all the same, Amy,' Reid said rather drily, 'but I'm having an early night.'

Amy pouted deliciously. 'You could regret it,' she said huskily.

Nyree tensed as some sixth sense told her Reid would retaliate this time as only he could. She was not wrong.

'Oh, I'm sure my loss will be someone's gain,' he drawled, and there was no mistaking his meaning.

A flash of pure temper lit Amy's beautiful eyes but it was gone in an instant. 'Enjoy your *domesticated* evening then, darling,' she said lightly and wafted away.

Reid stared after her for a moment then sat down looking as if he'd like to strangle someone. 'Stupid little bitch,' he said harshly.

Nyree was silent.

'No comment?' he asked her, still looking remarkably savage.

She shook her head.

'Then let's go for a walk or something,' he said impatiently—almost as if it was all her fault.

It was cold on the beach as they walked by the light of a million stars. Nyree had her new grey shoes in her hand but Reid hadn't bothered to remove his, and the sand was fairly firm. They walked in silence up to the rocky point that divided Fisherman's Beach from tiny Shelving Beach.

Occasionally Nyree tried to think of something to say to break the silence, but each time she stole a glance at his grim, shuttered face, and held her peace.

But he spoke as they turned back. 'The unfortunate thing about women is that one needs them from time to time. I don't suppose you'd be that . . . *impartial* and accommodating, Miss Westbrook?'

CHAPTER FOUR

IT TOOK about five seconds for his meaning to sink in.

Then Nyree gasped, swung round and raised her free hand to hit him with all her might. But he caught her wrist and said with soft, mocking amusement, 'I wouldn't advise that. I'm sure the saying big is beautiful applies most aptly to you, my dear, but I happen to be bigger.'

'You . . . you . . .' Sheer fury made it impossible to speak but it didn't prevent her from raising her other hand still with her shoes in it, intent on inflicting God knew what damage with them. But he caught that wrist and tightened his grip on it until she was forced to drop them with a breathless little sound of pain.

'Sorry,' he said, easing the pressure immediately, 'but you could have brained me or blinded me or both, with those heels.'

'Let me *go*!'

'In a minute.' He held her wrists in front of her in an unbreakable grip until she stopped struggling and glared at him scorchingly. 'If I gave you cause for offence . . .'

'Offence!' she hissed. 'You insulted me deliberately. *Twice*. Not that I care about your continual barbs about my height and . . . but,' she took a breath, 'to make me the object of your all-time cynicism towards women simply because I happen to be one and simply

80

because I happen to be on hand—that's about as low as any man can go in my book! And ...'

'That's not altogether true,' he broke in with his lips twisting wryly.

'Oh yes, it is!' she flung at him. 'All right, so your wife might have given you some cause to be this way, and your overbearing mother—and dear Amy might have left a bitter taste in your mouth—but to ...'

She stopped as he laughed softly then murmured, 'You should have been a psychologist instead of a teacher, Nyree ... Don't.' He looked at her enigmatically as she struggled again briefly. 'I have no intention of hurting you,' he added mildly.

'You're hurting my freedom,' she said bitterly. 'You have no right ...' She closed her eyes and tried to steady her breathing.

'I'll let you go when I've said what I want to say. At least allow me to ... acquit myself of one charge. It had occurred to me that I'd like to go to bed with you before I said what I said just now ... and I accept that I phrased it badly.'

Nyree went still, her eyes wide now and dark.

'That surprises you?' He let go of her wrists suddenly.

She staggered then went quite still. And finally she said uncertainly—and could have killed herself for the uncertainty, 'Is that what you call ... acquitting yourself?'

'Perhaps. Doesn't it?' He studied her dazed face carefully.

'I don't see ...'

'I mean, doesn't it make it something ... personal as

opposed to just picking on you simply because you're to hand? The fact that after our tennis match when you were tired but relaxed, after we'd tested each other and enjoyed it both physically and mentally, I thought how . . . pleasurable it would be to finish the encounter in the one place we might really be equal?'

Nyree moved in protest but he went on.

'I thought of starting to make love to you very slowly while we recouped our strength, I thought of how you'd moved on the court and what it would be like to have that magnificent, lithe body naked and quiescent beneath my hands, beneath me . . . But I also thought that you wouldn't stay quiet for very long, that you would participate because that's the way things are between us and . . .'

'Stop it,' she whispered. 'I . . . we barely know each other!' She put her hands to her face gripped by a new kind of agitation.

He said slowly, 'In some ways I think we know each other rather well. It may only have been four days but we've virtually been living together. We've fought and made up, you've adopted my cause and because of that I've told you . . . more than I've ever told anyone. But of course, if what I was thinking didn't occur to you . . .?'

'No,' she said quickly, too quickly perhaps so she took a ragged breath and said it again, 'No. It's . . . it's unthinkable. And there's Si . . . oh!' She broke off and peered at her watch distractedly. 'It's ten to ten, we have to get back!'

But he didn't stir. 'I wasn't proposing to embarrass Simon, if that's what you thought,' he said coolly. 'In fact I wasn't going to . . .'

'Please, don't say any more,' she begged. 'Let's just forget it. Please.'

She thought, as she held her breath, that he was either going to laugh at her or demolish her verbally. He did neither. After a time he just shrugged, bent down to pick up her shoes and said, 'Don't forget *these*.'

At midnight, Nyree was still awake, lying in bed and staring at nothing in the dark.

She lay still for a while longer, then with a sigh reached for the other pillow to prop herself up a bit more. The green of her nightgown glimmered palely and she had left her hair loose so that it lay on her shoulders.

But although she'd been lying so quietly and staring at nothing in particular, her mind was anything but quiet, because she had acknowledged, not long after coming to bed and finding sleep impossible, that she had lied.

Lied to Reid Matthews when she had denied certain thoughts after their tennis match. Only it was worse in a sense because she had denied them to herself, refused to allow them to surface. But when he had spoken his thoughts aloud, it had been as if she'd glanced into a mirror and seen the reflection of her subconscious. And panicked—yes, panicked, she mused desolately. But how did it happen? I thoroughly disliked him, I still dislike a lot of his sentiments, I . . . How did it happen? she asked herself helplessly. Because we have been like a family and . . . I was more lonely than

I realised? It can't have been that altogether. Because . . . he's dangerously attractive to women—is that what I've fallen for?

'Dangerous,' she whispered, holding on to that thought stubbornly. 'Well, why not . . . If anything he's more cynical than I am, he's . . . he can be so nice and then say things like—"the unfortunate thing about women is that you need them from time to time".' She winced as she remembered. 'But I think he knows women well and how to please them so that you could fall in love happily and then live to regret it . . . no!'

She sat up abruptly and realised she was sweating but cold at the same time. 'No, it's not that,' she told herself. 'It's a physical attraction, but instead of falling on the stony ground that is usually me, it found some cracks—some weakness. If you care to remember, Nyree, it was not long after your father died that Brad . . . And Simon hasn't helped, he really got to you . . . *that's* why you're vulnerable, that and because you've been remembering how long you've been alone . . .'

The next morning, to add to her fears—how could it be possible to be normal; how would *he* be?—Nyree discovered she was not only heavy-eyed but slightly stiff.

Stiff! she thought indignantly. I can't understand it. It's not as if . . . well, I haven't played tennis but I've hardly been still for a moment, walking, climbing, swimming, sailing—I must have played even harder than I realised. Which just goes to show what a fool you are, Nyree Westbrook, she told herself sharply. You had better be more ... alert! About a whole lot of things.

Simon knocked on the interconnecting door then and called through that they were ready for breakfast and starving and was she ready, and she tensed before calling back that she was.

But there was nothing to embarrass her. Reid looked at her fleetingly but acutely and then was perfectly natural—which irritated her obscurely. And if she was stiff, in manner, in those first few moments, Simon was still bubbling over with the beach barbecue of the previous evening and seemed not to notice.

And finally, half-way through breakfast, she found herself actually laughing with Reid Matthews, cynic, womaniser, destroyer of sleep amongst other things.

It came about when Simon suggested an expedition to Long Beach. 'It's not a very long walk.'

'*Walk*?' his father and Nyree said simultaneously and in patent tones of disapproval.

It had been impossible not to laugh. 'Stiff?' Reid queried. 'I am.'

She nodded ruefully.

'Simon, how about a quiet morning on the beach? Nyree and I are rather feeling our age this morning,' he said gravely.

'What does that mean?'

'That we ... er ... got carried away playing tennis yesterday.'

'My mother used to play tennis,' Simon said. 'She was very ...' He stopped. 'Sometimes I can't remember her *face* even when I look at her picture. It doesn't seem real ...' He stopped again and turned away but not before his face crumpled and his voice had clogged with tears.

Reid sat up and Nyree held her breath but Simon had already stumbled to his feet and was going. Reid was not far behind, however.

They were away all morning.

Nyree lay on the beach, too tense to do anything else, too tired and too emotional, which no amount of talking to herself seemed to ease.

Then a long shadow dropped down beside her. Reid.

'Oh!' She sat up. 'You're back. Is he all right?'

'Yes. More or less. He spotted Dean on a surf ski.'

'Where did you go?'

'Long Beach,' he said wryly. 'And it's quite a walk but if anything it's even more beautiful than Leeke or Butterfish. And for the first time we were able to talk about Sylvia. I told him how we'd met, all the little things I remembered. I tried to explain again what had happened but mostly ... we remembered and it seemed to give us some ... common ground at least.'

Nyree couldn't speak but she touched his hand briefly.

'God knows I've tried before.'

'I know.' She cleared her throat. 'Sometimes there's a ... right time, that's all.'

He was silent, staring out to sea. 'A right time and a right place. There was no one over there and the water was so clear it was unbelievable and the sky was so big and the beach ... and the bush was so still. It really came home to me that I *had* to forge a link between the two of us, and how to do it. That to remember Sylvia with malice was like . . . denying a part of Simon, that my memories had been just as much a bar to getting closer to him—as his had. I think I managed to change that.'

Nyree stared at him. He was still staring out to sea with a frown between his eyes—and the strangest thing happened to her. In the space of a split second she found herself wanting to smooth away that frown, wanting to comfort him, to hold him in her arms and more, but not merely wondering about it as had happened yesterday, this time most intimately wanting it, and her body quivered beneath a primitive onslaught of desire that all but took her breath away and mentally made her reel with shock.

'What is it?' he said, turning his head and encountering her fixed, green gaze.

'N . . . nothing!' she forced herself to say. 'I think I'll have a swim.' She got up abruptly and ran down to the water's edge and plunged straight in.

It was colder than a cold shower at first which caused her some grim amusement. But at least after ten minutes of vigorous swimming she felt restored to some sanity and even confident that she could face him again, although she dearly wished she didn't have to.

He was sitting propped up against a wooden fence post chewing a blade of grass from the lawn behind the fence as she walked up, bent down for her towel and wrapped herself in it sarong-wise. Little droplets of water clung to the smooth skin of her shoulders and legs and pitted the sand as she raised her hands to wring out her hair.

'I think . . .'

'Nyree . . .'

They stopped and she looked down at him properly for the first time, into the blue of his eyes regarding her so steadily. He knows, she thought immediately, and flinched inwardly. I don't know how but he knows . . .

She launched into speech. 'I think I'll get changed for lunch—it must be nearly lunch time and I'm too wet to put my clothes over my costume. Oh . . .' The lunch announcement came over the loudspeaker system. 'You and Simon go ahead. I'll join you. I'm sure you won't have to wait for Simon.' She bent down again and gathered up her things. 'See you,' she said huskily and walked away without a backward glance.

For someone who had not been able to sleep the previous night because of all the conflicting thoughts she had entertained about Reid Matthews and herself, she found her mind was curiously blank as she let herself into her room, showered briefly and dressed in khaki culottes and a crisp white cotton blouse.

But she stopped as she plaited her hair and stared at herself in the mirror and did wonder where the confidence and serenity of her expression had fled to, because all she could see in her eyes was a shadow of the shock she had experienced on the beach. I never dreamt I could . . . lose control like that, she thought. How . . . how did this happen? Thank God there are only two more days left.

Lunch on Keppel was a feast, a *smorgasbord* of hot dishes, cold meat, sea food and salad. It was always a problem to make a choice. Today, Nyree had little trouble, though. Her appetite seemed to have deserted her and there was not much on her plate as she sat down at the table where Reid and Simon were already half-way through their lunch.

'Thought you might have decided to give lunch a miss,' Reid said casually but with a fleeting glance at her rather bare-looking plate, and a straight, acute one right into her green eyes.

She looked away defensively.

'Try a glass of wine,' he said quietly and poured her one from the carafe he had ordered.

She hesitated then shrugged and murmured her thanks. It was a Moselle, cool and clean on her palate, and just that first sip seemed to steady her. She smiled at Simon, and decided to concentrate on him. But, being Simon, he was not easy to read.

'Two things have come up,' Reid said, pushing his plate away and leaning back in his chair. 'The Keppel Kids Klub . . .'

'Why do they spell everything with a K, Dad?' Simon piped up. 'They have a Kricket Klub as well.'

'To go with Keppel, I presume,' Reid said humourlessly.

'I thought they couldn't spell at first!' Simon grinned at his father and Nyree's heart bumped. They have . . . oh, I think he has got through at last . . .

'The Keppel Kids Klub,' Reid went on, 'has a fun bush walk planned for this afternoon and Dean and Simon have decided to go. The other thing is, Amanda and Harold are arriving this afternoon.'

Nyree blinked and put down her knife and fork and turned a slightly dazed gaze to Reid.

'I got the message about ten minutes ago,' he

murmured. 'Amanda is mobile now and—we're going to extend our stay for a couple of days.'

'Well, that's nice,' Nyree said uncertainly then tried to qualify it. 'But I . . .'

'We can talk about that later,' Reid said barely audibly. 'Eat your lunch . . . OK, young Simon, I can see Dean approaching. Got all your gear? Hat and so on?'

'Yes.' Simon slipped off his chair excitedly but didn't forget his manners. 'Excuse me, Nyree. Do you mind . . .?'

'Of course not. Enjoy yourself!' she managed to say lightly. But a few moments after he had gone she pushed her plate away unfinished and reached for her glass. 'They do a good job with the kids here, don't they,' she said into the awkward silence.

'Yes.' He sounded abrupt. 'Nyree . . .'

But she pushed out her chair and stood up. 'I think I'll have a rest this afternoon. Perhaps . . . perhaps I've had too much sun because I feel really tired. Do you mind if I desert you too?'

He looked up at her steadily then stood up himself. 'I'll walk with you.'

'Oh, no! I . . .'

'Don't argue,' he gave her a little push, 'I'm coming.'

He came—all the way—and when she unlocked her door and turned to him rather helplessly, he took the key out of the lock, gave her another little push, followed her in and closed the door behind them.

'Look,' she said, some colour entering her cheeks and some spirit her eyes.

'No, you look,' he said evenly. 'We can't leave things

like this. It's ridiculous. We're two adults, two *experienced* adults and we should be able to talk things out.'

'There would have been nothing to "talk out" if you hadn't . . .' She stopped abruptly as he raised an ironic eyebrow, and she turned away angrily.

'Wouldn't there?'

She tried to ignore the question. She walked over to the glass door that led to the balcony and stared out over the gardens to the sea.

'Wouldn't there, Nyree?' His voice was low but insistent, and it tormented her until she whirled back, her green eyes suddenly blazing, and said intensely, 'Don't do this to me! Don't . . .' She broke off just as suddenly, biting her lip and knowing she had set the seal on giving herself away. She closed her eyes in exasperation. 'It's . . . impossible,' she said dully then. 'You must know that—better than I do, probably.'

'Perhaps,' he said very quietly. 'And perhaps that's why I have to explain at least.' Her lashes fluttered up and she saw that he had moved quite close to her, and that his eyes were very blue and very sombre. 'I haven't been very fair to you, have I? And that's something I don't want to have on my conscience.'

'Explain what?' she whispered.

'What happened last night. I . . . it was not something I intended to mention. How . . . I'd thought of you. Not so much because we barely know each other or because it's in any way impossible for it to have happened but because in some—important ways, we know each other too well. I think that's what you really meant when you said it was impossible just now.'

She could only stare at him.

'But last night, after losing my temper and—allowing my prejudices to speak for themselves,' he said, 'I . . . realised you were the last person I wanted to hurt . . . like that, and that only the truth would—wipe out my insults. So I *thought*. I can see now that all I've done with the truth is create a minor hell for you.'

How could she lie when he had hit the nail on the head so accurately? She nodded, a spare little movement of her head.

'Because,' he paused, 'I can guess anyway. Tell me about him,' he said abruptly.

Her lips parted.

'I've told *you* everything,' he said impatiently. 'And you're not a fool. You must have been able to tot it all up and arrive at the conclusion that I'm not a great believer in love and marriage. It certainly hasn't been very difficult for me to work out that something like this happened to you once before. Why else, me aside, would you go around most of the time as if you'd entered a nunnery?'

Her eyes flashed. 'You . . .'

' Oh, come on,' he said wearily, 'it takes one to know one.'

'I'm sure the last thing you contemplated was taking a vow of chastity,' she said bitterly.

'Did you do that?'

'*No*. You said it . . .'

'No?'

'I . . . oh, God . . .' She put her knuckles to her mouth and took a shuddering breath.

'I meant,' he grasped her wrists, but gently and with

his voice suddenly gentler too, 'it takes someone who's been hurt to recognise another. Tell me about him.' He bore her hands down to her waist and waited.

'He was married,' she said blindly.

'You *knew* that?' He looked at her incredulously.

'No. He told me he was divorced but he was only separated. It hadn't happened.'

'Who was he?'

She pulled her wrists free. 'My Science lecturer at University.'

'Older?'

'Yes. About twelve years. But then you're . . .' She stopped and bit her lip.

'There's a difference. You're not a naïve, starry-eyed little girl now,' he said with irony.

'I was never little,' she said, matching his irony.

'Young then . . .'

'I'm not sure I was naïve.'

'I think we all are until it happens to us for the first time,' he observed. 'But perhaps I can phrase it better.' He narrowed his eyes. 'Yes . . . quite mature for your age in some ways, perhaps a little uncomfortable with boys of your own age because of your close relationship with your father and a wider education but still . . . deliciously young to a jaded married man.'

Nyree winced and turned away.

'Something like that?' he queried.

She could only shrug in acknowledgement.

'Would you like a cup of coffee?' he asked then, taking her by surprise.

'All . . . all right. I'll . . .'

'No, I'll make it,' he said authoritatively. 'Sit down.'

He made the coffee and brought it over and sat down opposite her. 'What happened?'

She glanced at him over the rim of her cup. 'It was strange,' she said slowly. 'I think he and his wife were drifting down the path towards divorce almost ... blindly. I think, to give him credit, he really loved his children and didn't want to lose them. I think they might have drifted in that state for ages while it was their own differences that kept them apart. They were sort of ... immutable.'

'What do you mean?'

'Not prepared to give an inch. But then, when she found out about me—I don't know—perhaps she came down to earth with a bump. Perhaps she realised they'd sort of ... only been playing a game, but with another woman on the scene, it could all become stark reality. She needn't have worried.' Her lips curled.

'All the same, she set out to get him back?'

'Yes. I ... I can't blame her.'

He was silent. Then he said, 'How did you find out?'

'I had to be hit over the head with it.' Nyree closed her eyes at the remembered shock and pain. 'I must have been ... besotted,' she said grimly, 'not to have questioned the delays, the time he spent away from me when there was no reason. I ... in the end, she told me that he was a married man. Because he was a lecturer, we'd kept it all very quiet and that fitted in well for him. I still can't believe ...'

'Don't,' Reid said. 'It's futile and it can happen to any of us. What did you do?'

'I stopped seeing him immediately,' Nyree said. 'But because I only had three months of my degree to go, I couldn't avoid him completely without throwing it all away. And one day he cornered me and tried to explain. I . . . That I could have borne.' She put her cup down and studied her hands. 'I mean, that he had been genuinely torn between us. But when he suggested . . .' She couldn't go on.

'That he could have his cake and eat it—keep his family intact and still have you?' Reid suggested flatly.

'Yes. I could have killed him. I can't describe how I felt.' She breathed deeply and raked a hand through her hair.

'And you swore never to let that happen to you again? That whatever the cost you'd stay away from men?'

She sighed and had to smile faintly. 'I didn't precisely swear it. But it caught up with me all the same, I suppose. Nor did I realise what . . . a grip it had on me.'

'Until you met me.'

'Yes.' She stood up and paced around the room restlessly for a time. Then she said, 'I did think the same as you, yesterday—and today it was much worse. Which you knew, somehow or other didn't you? But I think there are explanations for it, such . . .'

'Oh, I'm sure there are,' he interrupted. 'We started out hating each other and ended up wanting each other.'

She flinched.

'You can't accept that?' he queried.

She stopped pacing and her lips trembled as she faced him. 'No. I mean I can accept it,' she said but there was a flicker of doubt in her eyes, 'that I . . .' She grimaced and shrugged.

'You don't believe I could want you?' He sounded harsh and he stood up. She backed away a step but their gazes clashed. 'There's only one way I can prove it, you know,' he said ironically. 'Care to let me try?'

'*No!*' She backed away further and her eyes glittered with sudden tears. Unfortunately she backed into a chair and would have fallen if he hadn't reached her in a couple of strides and pulled her into his arms. 'Reid, let me go!' she panted and tried to break free. 'Don't . . .'

'I'm not going to,' he said roughly. 'What do you take me for? Calm down . . .' He broke off and closed his eyes briefly at the agonised look on her face. 'I shouldn't have said what I did—about proving anything.' He loosened his grasp but not enough to let her go. 'But I've got to make you *understand* somehow, Nyree. Look, if I valued you less . . . I could be exploring your body now and no doubt with exquisite pleasure. But where would we go from there?'

She had quietened while he spoke but now she shivered and he drew her closer again and laid his cheek on her hair. 'It's not,' he said and his voice was deep but very quiet, 'only what happened to me that's made me this way—so sceptical about love and marriage. It's what I've seen in others too. I saw my mother drive my father into a . . . shell of himself. I suppose you could say it's something I've grown up with and it's made me a lousy candidate for it. Which is why, for someone like you—honest, caring and beautiful as well, oh yes, I'm the last person to be pinning any hopes on. It would be a terrible way to repay you for what you've done for Simon—and then there is the problem of Simon and how he would react to a stepmother. Although in that respect . . .' He stopped.

Nyree leant against him because it was impossible not to, and impossible not to feel the strength of his arms around her or not to let her mind take wings and imagine how it would be if they made love . . .

'We could . . .' she whispered then thought, oh God, did I say that? Could what? Marry for Simon's sake? Just pray he didn't hear—I shouldn't *be* in his arms thinking these things.

But he heard although he didn't quite understand. 'Could we?' He held her away from him. 'Have an affair—another secret affair?' His eyes probed hers unmercifully until she hid her face in his shoulder despairingly. 'Nyree, look at me,' he commanded softly then. And when she did at last, he said, 'You might never get me this honest again, certainly not when I'm holding you so close, but you deserve more, so much more. You deserve a husband and children. You're not going to find one this way, though,' he added with an effort.

'Not with you, I know.' She made herself say the words.

'I meant, by shutting yourself away from men. There has to be someone out there for *you*. Going into a sort of spiritual purdah isn't . . .'

He stopped as a little jolt of laughter that was closer to tears shook her. 'A nunnery, now purdah,' she murmured shakily. 'I'm not that bad.'

He said nothing.

'I'm not.' She looked at him defensively. 'Only a few days ago, before this.' She stopped then went on with a tinge of defiance, 'I thought of . . . I dreamt of being with a man, letting my hair down . . . oh, it sounds stupid but . . .'

'Tell me,' he insisted.

She told him. 'It was my silly daydream at Leeke's homestead and . . .' And when she finished her cheeks were pink and she said ruefully, 'I'm not usually so fanciful but it was all bound up with my pioneering dreams. It must prove I haven't quite gone into purdah though.'

'Yes,' he said softly. 'And I think you would have made some pioneer a marvellous wife, been their inner strength and joy. Which is all the more reason why I can't . . . do this. And all the more reason why you shouldn't settle for anything less. It can still happen—for you.' He bent his head and kissed her gently.

And with a shuddering little sigh, she kissed him back then pulled away. He let her go.

'I . . . it would be better if I could go, today. I might even be able to get on to the four o'clock flight only . . .' Her shoulders slumped.

'Only what?' he queried broodingly.

'I'd feel awful about leaving without saying goodbye to Simon.'

'Then don't.'

'Reid,' she said his name imploringly, 'I can't stay on with you . . . all.'

A nerve flickered in his jaw. 'If you went tomorrow morning, it would only be one day sooner than you . . . we were supposed to go. Simon would find that easier to understand and you'd able able to say goodbye to him properly. I'm sure it would mean a great deal to him, and to me ... But perhaps I have no right to ask you that after the things I've done and said.'

'I ...' she took a breath, 'appreciate the things you've said ... and not done. One day,' she tried to smile, 'I'll even be grateful. The eleven o'clock flight tomorrow will be fine. Could you ...?'

'Yes. I'll fix it,' he said sombrely. 'What are you going to do now?'

'I'm going to have that rest I promised myself. I ...' But her voice wound down and they stared at each other.

'I think I'll say my goodbyes now, in private then.' He took her hands into his. 'I only wish I was the right one for you, my lovely Amazon. Take care,' he said, pulling her into his arms and holding her close for a moment. 'Take care ...'

Then he released her abruptly and walked out, through the outside door.

Nyree stood quite still where he had left her, listening to his footsteps going down the stairs. Then she moved so that she could see out over the balcony but without being seen from below. And she watched him walk through the gardens and on to the beach.

She watched him walk along the beach until he was out of sight. Then she buried her face in her hands.

She slept for hours then stayed in her room packing, and when that was done, she watched the sunset alone, her last on Great Keppel, and whether it was her imagination or not she wasn't sure, but it was the most splendid, beautiful one she had seen yet. Beautiful and haunting enough to bring rare tears to her eyes. She watched until the last shimmer of violet left the water and the last ray of light left the sky.

Then she turned away, closed her eyes and took a deep breath. And started to dress for dinner.

Getting through the evening proved easier than she had expected, but then both Amanda and Harold Inchwood proved to be throughly nice and easy to fit in with. And Nyree could easily see the likeness to both his vivacious, attractive aunt and his father in Simon.

And it helped her heavy heart to see Simon looking perceptibly happy, although he had expressed his disappointment that she couldn't finish off the holiday with them all.

After dinner, in a lull in the conversation, she suggested she should take Simon to bed. Amanda protested, saying it was Nyree's last night and wouldn't she like to let loose a little, but Reid broke in and said that Nyree and Simon had established a bedtime ritual which he thought they both enjoyed.

Perhaps, Nyree thought, Amanda had detected the unspoken constraint in the air, because she glanced at her brother, then she smiled her warm smile and left it at that.

Both Harold and Reid stood up as they left the table and Simon said his goodnights, but Reid walked to the door of the restaurant with them.

'Night, Dad,' Simon said and started to go, then he turned back and hugged his father impulsively.

Nyree watched them and when Simon did step out

into the night this time, her green eyes were suspiciously bright as Reid straightened.

Their gazes caught and held until Reid said very quietly, 'Are you all right?'

She swallowed the lump in her throat. 'Yes. And very *happy* for you both. Goodnight.'

They read together for their last bedtime until Simon started to yawn and she said, 'We'll be needing matchsticks to prop your eyes open soon, young man!'

'Mmm,' he agreed sleepily. 'I still wish you could stay for the rest of the time, Nyree.'

'So do I, Simon, but you don't need me now.'

'We could just be friends. That's what we've been since we met, haven't we?'

'Yes, we have.'

'I was a bit worried about you,' he confessed. 'I didn't know what to expect.'

Nyree smiled down at him. 'I didn't know what to expect either.' She slipped her hand into his. 'But if I had a son . . .' She stopped and changed tack swiftly. 'How would it be if I gave you a memento from one good friend to another? Would you like to keep this book?'

'Oh, yes!' he said eagerly. 'Then I'd always have something to remember you by. Could you write something to me in it?'

She got up and fetched her pen and wrote on the fly-leaf—'To Simon—Thank you for being such a good friend and I'll always remember our holiday. Nyree.'

He read it enthusiastically then his face fell. 'But I haven't got anything for you.'

'Remember this?' She disappeared into her room again and came back with the peacock feather he had found. 'That'll be my memento of you.'

That seemed to satisfy him and he started to look sleepy again. Then he said out of the blue, 'My dad told me about my mother this morning. We talked about her. She doesn't seem so far away now. I was so afraid I would forget her but he said he would always help me to remember. He . . . I didn't want to like him because I thought he hated her. And if he hated her . . .'

'Mothers and fathers sometimes have problems, Simon,' she interposed quietly, 'but that doesn't mean they don't love their children and I think your Dad loves you very much even if he hasn't known you for very long—I know he does.'

'Did he tell you?'

'Yes, he did.'

Simon's face relaxed then he threw his arms around her neck and hugged her fiercely for a moment. 'Goodnight, Nyree.'

Just another few minutes, Nyree thought the next morning at about eleven. Then it will all be over. Thank God, I don't think I can stand much more.

It was warm and sunny standing beside the small airport terminal as the arriving passengers streamed off the Sunstate Air Twin Otter that had just landed. Inside the terminal they would be greeted with a glass of an exotic tropical punch and divided into two groups each to be escorted to their accommodation by a resort guide.

And as she watched, Nyree marvelled at the hand of

fate. Thirteen days ago she and Simon had been among a similar happy throng and she had been supremely unaware of what lay before her.

She looked away, over the sweep of the cricket oval, but her gaze fell on the tennis courts and she switched it back abruptly to look down at herself. She was wearing comfortable beige cord pants, a brown blouse and carrying a warm brown and red and white tweed checked jacket. It would be colder in Brisbane. Her hair was tied back with a red ribbon—and Reid was standing beside her in shorts and a T-shirt with a floppy white hat in his hands. Standing silently, tall and tanned and with his blue eyes resting on Simon who was hanging over the fence watching the aircraft being unloaded and loaded with luggage.

'I . . .' Nyree said and stopped, her restless gaze falling on a family group leaving the terminal in the wake of a guide. Two children in their early teens, a willowy woman with dark, curly hair and a man, looking slightly weary—but then he had always had that look and Nyree had grown to love it. Or so she'd thought.

Her lips parted on a little gasp of surprise and she turned away abruptly. But Reid heard her and moved his head to look at her enquiringly.

'Nothing,' she said hastily.

'You look as if you've seen a ghost.' He glanced over his shoulder with a faint frown but Nyree saw with a quick glance herself that all the arriving guests were now obscured by trees and shrubbery as they followed their guides.

Then she saw with relief that passengers were boarding the aircraft and she turned to Reid and put out her hand. She even managed to smile calmly as she said, 'Goodbye. Take care of yourself and Simon. He mentioned his mother to me last night. He seems much less confused now.'

Her long, elegant hand rested in his larger one and their eyes met, hers green and faintly shadowed although her smile was still serene.

'Nyree . . .'

But Simon saved her. He came up with his farewells and she ruffled his fair hair, shook his hand and said she knew not what. Then at last she was free, walking through the gate and across the airfield to the plane. She looked back only once and waved at the top of the steps.

The plane took off up the hill and over Long Beach. Nyree stared out of the window as they banked to fly back over the island. Great Keppel, she thought, with its incredibly beautiful beaches, where everything that could possibly be spelt with a K was, a great place to get wrecked. How true . . .

CHAPTER FIVE

'WELL, well!' Gwen Foster said. 'So they're *all* up there now with the little boy. I must say I was rather impressed with Reid Matthews when he came to see me. Fine type of a man.' She rolled her eyes briefly. 'Perhaps he'll think soon of providing the child with a stepmother and a proper home. Seems odd that he never married again but then again, maybe it was lucky he didn't! Well, Nyree. I'm sure you did your usual excellent job, but to be quite honest you look a little tired. Was he a handful?'

'Not Simon,' Nyree said then bit her lip.

Gwen cocked a curious eye at her.

'I didn't sleep very well last night, that's all,' Nyree murmured.

'I always have that problem,' Gwen said understandingly. 'One has to be reorientated, doesn't one? So, you've still got a few days of holiday left, haven't you? The private schools don't go back until next week. Interested in any work?'

'No,' Nyree said slowly and uncertainly, because perhaps work was the answer. She had thought she needed to be alone but after last night . . .

'You don't sound too sure,' Gwen prompted.

'I know.' She looked rueful. 'I *must* be disorientated. Uh . . .' She stopped as a sudden thought hit her. 'No,' she said with decision. 'I think I'll go away on the boat

105

for a while. I might just cruise down to the Gold Coast.'

'Lucky you,' Gwen said enviously. 'All right, I'll strike you out until you get in touch with me. How's that? By the way, would you recommend Great Keppel for a holiday?'

Nyree stared at her. Not for fools like me, she thought. But she said, 'Definitely.'

Back at her flat on the top floor of a block of twelve, in a green, leafy suburb of Brisbane, she thought she felt better.

It was an older building but kept in good repair, and unlike more modern blocks, the rooms were quite large and airy. She had one bedroom, a study, and a combined lounge-dining-area. She had originally rented it furnished, if you could call a double bed, two lounge chairs, a minuscule dining-room table and not much else furnished. But she had gradually replaced and added to the original furniture except for the double bed, and she had bought a new mattress for that. Six months ago, she had had the flat painted ivory with white trims throughout. The ivory complemented her cane lounge suite with its deep, comfortable cushions covered in a pink-tinged tan linen. And pinks, tans and browns were the main colours in the geometric patterns of the dhurrie rug on the floor. Her dining-room setting was cane too, with a round glass-topped table and an unusual filigree brass lamp suspended from the ceiling above it. Two tall bookcases, both full, stood at either end of the room and beside the one in the lounge end was a low set of shelves supporting her television set, stereo and stacks of records.

But if the lounge was attractive but comfortable, her bedroom was almost austere. The bed was covered with a quilted cotton bedspread in a tiny all-over pattern of pale mistletoe-green on grey. The carpet was pale grey, there was a dark, short-ladder-back chair in one corner, a matching wood bedside table with a lamp and photo of her father and mother on it and that was all. The cupboards were built in and concealed behind white painted louvred doors. She used the vanity unit in the bathroom as a dressing-table and because the bathroom got an extra amount of light, she had a wrought-iron stand of pot plants in it and some more hanging from the ceiling. She rather thought her bathroom would look good in *House & Garden*, both sections.

Normally her flat gave her a feeling of security and achievement and independence and she took pleasure in the small things she could afford—small but expensive. Such as good linen, some fine china and glassware and a small but growing collection of rare books.

Normally, she thought, the day after she had arrived home from Keppel. Then she reminded herself that several moments ago, she had decided she felt better. And decided that some days of sailing on Moreton Bay and the Gold Coast Broadwater would complete the cure. It *had* to. What future was there in believing she had met a man and fallen in love with him in the space of a few days? A man who didn't want her moreover, a man who was dangerously cynical but who had been entirely honest with her . . .

'Only that made me fall more . . . no,' she whispered to herself. 'But I wonder what there is about me that men find they can resist? Not that Brad . . . yes he did. She looked happy, his wife. He looked just the same. I hope they are happy now. As for Reid, perhaps these things creep up on dedicated man-haters—*did* I become one? But then we each choose our own form of protection against hurt . . . Yes. Look at it that way. Hasn't Reid done it too?'

Fortunately, her philosophising saw her through the next couple of days which proved to be frustrating in other directions.

Her father had been too good a teacher and a sailor for her to take out a boat that had been lying moored for months without checking it out throughly. This was just as well because the bilge pump worked intermittently, then stopped working at all. It took a full afternoon to trace the problem to an electric switch and have it repaired. In the meantime both batteries which generated the power had gone flat and had to be replaced. Then, not to be outdone, the weather turned exceedingly stormy and the coastguard reported waves of over a metre and a half in Moreton Bay, and strongly advised against venturing out.

But finally things began to go her way and she got home at five one afternoon, dirty and tired but satisfied that the boat was shipshape, that the weather was clearing and that she would be off the next morning.

She had a bath, dressed in a loose paisley peasant

blouse with long sleeves over a pair of jeans and tied her hair in a frivolous knot on top of her head. Then she poured herself a glass of sherry, put the sound-track of *Amadeus* on the stereo and curled up on the settee. Daylight was fading fast but at least the sky was clear, and the only lamp she had on was the one above the dining-table, spattering soft patterns of light on the walls.

It was during the lovely Piano Concerto in E flat that someone rang her doorbell. She blinked, drifted back to earth from the melody, wondered who it could be, and reluctantly went to answer it.

It was Reid standing on her doorstep with his hand raised to ring again. Reid, casually dressed in grey slacks and a midnight-blue sweater over a white shirt—Reid, somehow taller than she remembered, bigger but as tanned and good-looking and ...

'You!' she said incredulously, angrily.

'Me,' he agreed. 'May I come in?'

'*No*. What for? This is ...' she sought for the right words, 'unnecessary ...' but that didn't sound right, 'ridiculous ... oh, just go away! We've said it all and the last thing ...' She stopped and gritted her teeth.

A flicker of amusement lit his eyes then faded. 'That's the point, I don't think we have quite said it all. That's why I'm here. You see, I happen to have spent the last couple of days more or less in the company of your ex-lover, Nyree.'

Her lips parted and her eyes were suddenly stunned—and he waited and watched her impassively.

'H-how,' she licked her lips and made an effort to get her voice working better, 'did you know?'

'If you let me in I'll tell you.'

'I . . .'

'Or I could make you, but I'd rather not,' he said without emphasis.

Her eyes flashed him a look of magnificent scorn, then she looked down and saw that he already had a foot in the doorway. She hesitated briefly, then with a bitter little shrug walked away from the door.

He came in, closed the door behind him and followed her through to the lounge where she stood for a moment with her head bent, as if gathering her suspended wits. Then she looked up and their gazes clashed across the room.

'How did I know?' he said quietly. 'I . . .'

'It doesn't matter,' she broke in.

'I think it does. I knew something had happened to you in those last few minutes before you left. You went quite white. But it was Amanda and Harold who were instrumental in unravelling the mystery, actually. Harold knows Bradley Enfield quite well—they're both in the same field, after all and Harold maintains contact with the Queensland University Science Faculty. In fact they've given us a lot of help over the years. So it wasn't unnatural to share a table with them for meals, go on expeditions together—you know what it's like up there.'

'Yes. Yes,' she said. 'But that proves nothing.'

'Do I have to give you proof?' he asked with a trace of irony.

'You didn't . . . mention me?' Her expression was suddenly horrified.

He smiled grimly. 'Give me some credit . . . But I

didn't have to. I only had to piece it all together. Things like Amanda and Harold discussing the Enfields . . . oh, in their own concerned way, saying that five or was it six years ago the marriage had seemed to be on the rocks and wasn't it great to see them so happy now? Of discovering that they'd arrived on the flight you'd left on. Things like perceiving that beneath their happy appearance there were still some tensions between Brad and Marianne Enfield. Such as the wary look that came into her eyes whenever an attractive, unattached girl came into his orbit. The way when Simon mentioned you once, he stopped dead, then almost visibly came to the mental decision that it had to be a coincidence, Simon mentioning *that* name . . .'

'Don't go on,' Nyree said bleakly. 'Yes, it was him, for what it's worth, and yes, I did see them just before I left . . . I suppose I did get a shock. I *don't* see why it's any reason for you to be here, though.' She faced him defiantly.

'I came,' his blue gaze ran over her from head to foot, the taut straight line of her stance, the proud tilt of her head despite the loose wisps of hair about her face glinting almost gold in the soft lamplight, the outline of her full, heavy breasts beneath the paisley blouse unconstrained by a bra, 'I came,' he said again, 'because I couldn't help thinking of you having to leave like that, alone again and not only after what . . . we went through but with such a vivid reminder of the past. I came because I found I didn't want to be thinking of you alone and hurt . . .'

She was silent for a long time. Then she whispered, 'In other words, you came because you felt sorry for me. Thanks, but I'm . . . I'll be fine. I'm used to being alone, and as for hurt . . . that's something I'll *never* be again.' The words slipped out, surprising her not only because they expressed a sentiment torn from her innermost being, but also because she had said them so vehemently.

And her eyes widened almost fearfully, as he walked towards her and said intensely, '*That's* what I was afraid of.'

'Reid . . .' She licked her lips and backed away a step, staring desperately into his eyes as he came closer. 'There's nothing *you* can do. I . . . I . . . what I said I didn't . . .'

'Mean?' he queried. 'I think you meant every word of it. Which is insane, criminally insane. You're made for love and marriage and children.'

'How trite,' she flashed at him.

'No, it's not . . .'

'Well, what am I supposed to do then?' she queried sardonically. 'Put an advertisement in the paper—"Willing wife and mother available. Ring so-and-so"? Oh, and I could send them to you to check my references . . .'

'Stop it, Nyree,' he said tersely. 'But it's crazy to . . . to put yourself on ice because of one unhappy love affair.'

'Two, don't you mean?' she countered swiftly then coloured and looked away. 'As for putting myself on ice,' she added barely audibly, 'I thought I was amazingly forward a few days ago. *That's* when I should have put myself on ice. But,' a curious sense of pride fuelled her anger again, 'aren't you adopting a rather false position? Aren't you preaching a philosophy to me that you yourself don't believe in? I know you don't believe in marriage and it has to be at least *partly* because of what happened to you.'

'All the same,' he said drily, 'my beliefs and disbeliefs don't have to apply to you except where they . . . conflict. Nor do I—did I—have a longing in my heart as you have in yours. Daydreams mightn't be essentially realistic but there's got to be a germ of the reality you see in yourself, in them. Nor do I go out of my way to surround myself with other people's children like a frustrated spinster . . .'

This time she did it. She hit him in a flash of fury that gave her the momentum and gave him no chance to evade it.

The silence that followed was extra loud as the record player clicked off. And he did nothing for a moment or two as her hand sank back to her side stinging.

Then he drawled, 'Well, bingo! But that's a game two can play.' And in the second of stunned misunderstanding on Nyree's part, he reached for her almost leisurely.

'W-what do you mean?' she stammered, shocked at what she'd done.

'That when women resort to violence it's often a call to armed combat of a different kind. This kind.' And his arms locked around her.

'Don't you dare!' she panted, trying desperately to free herself. 'It was no such thing. You're just looking for an excuse to . . . to . . .'

'Perhaps,' he murmured, staring down into her

agonised eyes. 'I didn't think my baser instincts would survive another onslaught of you, Nyree, did I? I was right. Don't look so frantic.'

'I am frantic. It was the last thing . . .' Tears of frustration beaded her lashes and sparkled green in the lamplight.

'Was it?' He pulled her a little closer so that she was leaning against him but with her arms up between them. And he moved one hand up her back to curve round her shoulder.

Her lips trembled. 'Yes.' It was barely a breath of sound. 'But I probably over-reacted or—you touched a very raw nerve.'

He was silent, cupping her shoulder with the palm of his hand and massaging it through the thin material of her blouse. He said at last, 'I'm sorry, and I'm sorry for this too, but it seems inevitable.' And he bent his head and began to kiss her.

She resisted mutely but she had no real answer for the strength of his arms—or the unexpected gentleness of his lips. Then she tried to say something about the last thing she could do was accept his pity . . .

His mouth left the corner of hers. 'Pity be damned,' he said huskily. 'There is—and there has been almost from the beginning—a mutual desire. Which we decided to deny because it wasn't in our best interests, but I think it's gone past that now. It has for me . . .' He stopped and sighed. '*Your* best interest, let's be honest. If you want me to go, I'll go.'

Nyree swallowed and shivered suddenly so that he felt it and held her very close, but more like a father than a lover. And as they stood like that, she knew with a sudden aching certainty that she loved Reid Matthews, that she wanted him, but above all, she loved him and the way he had only ever been honest with her—and that she would never be able to deny it to herself again . So . . . where do I go from here? The thought slid across her mind. To a greater loneliness than I've ever known, ever imagined? It has to be that, now. Or . . . if a miracle has happened for me, could . . . couldn't it happen that my love might reach across and heal him? Why shouldn't I fight for him? Why shouldn't I . . .? He needn't know. I wouldn't make any claims, bind him with any chains—how could I anyway? But one day he might know there's more to this desire . . .

For ever afterwards she was to be amazed that she should have made that momentous decision so quickly, but the other way seemed to be curiously cowardly, and anyway, he started to put her away from him . . .

She put up a hand and touched the side of his face where there was still a red mark with her fingertips. 'Stay, please.'

'You . . .' he started to say but she transferred her fingers to his lips and whispered,

'I think I need to be kissed and loved, even if it is all an illusion. You were right, since I got back I've felt like the only person inhabiting this planet—really dangerously alone. But I promise I won't read anything more into it than you want, or rush off into a nunnery if . . . when it ends.'

'Oh God,' he said, 'you . . . you're . . .'

But she slipped her hands around the back of his head and drew it down until their lips met.

It was a slow searching kiss at first then it became more and more urgent and when they broke away, she was breathing as if she'd run a mile, and the room whirled before her eyes. She closed them and murmured his name and he pulled her back into his arms and it was as if her splendid body was made for them.

They kissed again with an intensity she hadn't believed possible and she could only lay her head helplessly on his shoulder when it was finished, exploring her tender, swollen lips with her tongue. Then he spoke and what he said caused her a little jolt of laughter. 'Have you ever made love standing up?'

'No . . . are we in imminent danger of that?' she asked still smiling.

'Imminent. But there are better ways.'

'Mmm.' She disengaged herself slowly but took his hand. 'Come . . .'

The bedroom was dark but she switched on the bedside lamp, hesitated then turned to face him.

'What?' he said softly and reached out to cup her cheek in his hand.

'Nothing,' she whispered, turning her head and kissing his palm. They stood like that for a moment, then he slid his hand round the back of her neck, drawing her forward until their foreheads were touching.

'I've been dying to undress you for . . . I was going to say months but it feels like it,' he said unsteadily. He took a breath and blew it so that the wisps of hair haloing her face fluttered. 'On a path beside a golf course—yes, although I'd have shot myself rather than admit it then . . . no. That's not quite true. I told myself it might be what you needed. And once or twice later I told myself the same thing. But it was on Leeke's Beach that I . . .' He stopped and grimaced ruefully.

'Tell me,' she whispered.

'I don't quite know how to say it. But that's when the prospect of . . . subduing all that militant feminism about you got rather muddled. In other words, instead of thinking—here's a sheila who needs a man to bring her back to earth . . . sorry that's crude and . . .'

'I don't suppose women escape generalising about men. Go on.'

'I thought—do they?'

'Oh, yes. Secretly we think we're miles ahead of you. We like to think of you as overgrown children but— what were you thinking on Leeke's Beach?'

'That I'd like to get to know you better, first.'

'Thanks.' She broke away grinning but he pulled her back and she came willingly. And they rested cheek to cheek for a time in a sort of laughing communication of the mind that helped her over the last barrier.

So that when he slipped his hands beneath her blouse, she didn't resist, just caught her breath. Then when he looked for an opening to take it off, she untied the strings at the neckline and crossed her arms to lift it up and pull it over her head. He helped her and the paisley blouse fluttered to the floor unnoticed.

He said something that she didn't catch and slid his hands around her waist beneath her arms, and she rested her hands in the crook of his elbows.

They stood like that in silence for an age, she thought, and the lamplight played on her naked skin, the golden sweep of her shoulders and arms, the paler skin of her rich, rounded breasts, the pale velvety pink of her nipples and generous aureola, the sleek spareness of her torso beneath the fulness above, disappearing into the waistband of her jeans. And as she stood there, accepting his scrutiny, her pulses began to beat heavily and a faint dew of sweat broke out on her brow. The fact that he was still fully clothed somehow heightened the sheer erotic sensuousness of the moment for her in a way she had never experienced before. So that a tremor of longing swept through her body, deeply and desperately physical, and her lashes fluttered and she tipped her head back and moaned low in her throat, unable to stand the suspense any longer.

She didn't have to. He said in a voice torn from him, 'Oh God, you're magnificent. Love me . . .'

She woke slowly with no idea of the time and at first only a hazy idea of the place. She had been sleeping on her stomach with her head pillowed on her arms, and after a minute or two, she turned her head towards the side of the bed and opened her eyes.

Reid was sitting there watching her. He had drawn up her ladder-back chair and was sitting astride it with his arms resting on the back and his chin resting on his arms. He had his trousers on but no shirt. His hair was ruffled, lying across his forehead and sticking up at the back, and there was a faint blue shadow on his jaw.

Their eyes met but he didn't smile. Instead he put out a hand and pushed aside the crisp, crumpled, snowy-white percale sheet down the length of her and drew his fingers down her body, slowly, lingeringly from her armpit down her side, over the curve of her bottom, down the smooth golden skin of her flank, his hand coming to rest at last on her ankle and curving possessively around it.

Then he looked back and his eyes said it all in a silent salute, and she knew that for her, too, there were no words to describe what had happened between them.

She closed her eyes briefly in silent acknowledgement.

Then she pushed herself up on one elbow, gathered her hair back with her free hand, realised belatedly that all she wore was her wrist-watch and reached for the sheet. 'Do you have to go now?'

A shadow crossed his eyes. 'No. Not unless you want me to.'

'No,' she said softly. 'But I thought, well . . .'

'As far as Simon and the others are concerned, I'm on my way to Melbourne for a conference.'

'Then . . .?' She looked at him questioningly.

'It's not *the* most important conference in the world and I thought you might be hungry when you woke up. We . . . missed dinner.'

'Oh!' she gasped, catching sight of the loaded tray on the bedside table suddenly.

'I didn't cook,' he said apologetically. 'I raided your fridge and your wine-rack though. Your fridge was rather well stocked.'

She sat right up adjusting the sheet under her arms and he picked up the tray and put it down on the side of the bed. There were two plates on it and on each, pink slices of ham cut from the bone, potato salad, lettuce and tomato, a serving each of rice salad with pineapple, mushrooms, bacon, prawns and capsicum, and a buttered roll each. From her wine rack he had chosen a bottle of Mateus Rosé and there were two crystal wine glasses gleaming in the light. The finishing touch was two furled pink linen napkins.

For a moment as she stared down at the tray, she was speechless, moved beyond words, and when she looked up at last her green eyes were suspiciously bright. But she blinked any hint of tears away and her lips curved into a smile. 'I'm *starving*.'

He grinned back and reached for the wine to open it. When each glass was full of the browny pink liquid, he raised his glass and she raised hers and they touched them together in a toast. Then he said. 'It's cold out here.'

'Come back to bed then.'

He came, adjusting the blanket and bedcover decorously first, and they ate with the tray between them on the covers, talking quietly. She told him why her fridge happened to be so well stocked—because she had prepared some food in advance for her sailing trip. Which led him to ask her more about her boat and what plans she'd had.

Then, when they had finished eating, he put the tray down on the floor and poured her another glass of wine. She curled up with it, facing him, and after a little silence he reached out and stroked her hair.

'So it's happened,' he said very quietly.

'Mmmm.' She sipped her wine and couldn't remember ever feeling more relaxed, more deliciously languid, soothed by the food and the wine, by the feeling of the sheet on her skin, by his presence and his hand on her hair. And she thought they might sleep again, as the silence lengthened, and when their glasses were empty and he took hers and put them down on the floor.

Then she discovered, curiously, that she didn't feel like sleeping, that that deliciously languid feeling was oddly deceptive . . .

She stirred, hesitated, then stroked the broad expanse of his chest with her fingertips. His hand stilled on her hair and she looked up into his eyes to see that his eyelids were half lowered, but not enough to mask the look in them that made her heartbeat trip suddenly and her fingers falter. But only briefly, and she let them wander over his skin, exploring, and she moved closer so that she could trail her lips down the side of his neck and across his shoulder, her hand now caressing his back. And all the time, as she was making this intimate exploration of his strong tall body, intertwining her legs with his, a deep well of desire was growing at the pit of her stomach.

Yet this time was different from the last. This time she was aware of the need to take it slowly, to savour it, and whether her need communicated itself to Reid, or whether they were simply of the same mind, she didn't know, but she gradually realised he was doing the same. He kissed her breasts while she stroked his legs with her toes. Then she wound her arms about his neck and teased his lips apart with her tongue while he crushed her to him about the waist.

She had never been a bold lover, she realised dimly and with some surprise, then forgot about it immediately, as she deliberately kept hold of her mounting excitement—and knew that he was as well, that they were testing each other, as they had a habit of, and that it was the most exquisite test . . .

Nor did she care in the end when she gave in first because it was a defeat that was also a victory—she was testing him to the limit too, she knew. And it was neither a victory nor a defeat when he was kneeling over her, lifting her hips to him and she was lying passively with her arms curved above her head, her hair spilling over them—and when she raised her hands suddenly and caught his shoulders and pulled him down to her and their bodies were joined in a breathtaking, shuddering union and the ultimate release.

'When do you have to go?'

She had woken first this time and lain quiet for a time, still shaken physically and mentally by the intensity of their lovemaking, and feeling curiously sober in the light of day. Then she had slipped out of bed, showered and dressed and cleared away their feast.

He had slept on, taking nearly all the bed, and with the pillows pushed everywhere, and with a little pang she had remembered how Simon had slept—at impossible angles and with his pillow nearly always on the floor . . . That's when she had said those words aloud but barely audibly, and known why her heart was heavy after the joy of last night. Because it wasn't going to be easy to lead a double life, to bind him with no chains, to watch him go and wonder . . . wonder if this was a fight she could win. But it has to be this way,

Nyree, she told herself. Let him go free.

She bit her lip and glanced around her bedroom, so chaste until last night, and went quietly away to make breakfast.

He must have woken up and padded through to the kitchen soundlessly because just as she was about to slide a perfect sunny-side-up egg on to a plate, she felt his arms slide around her waist.

She stopped with the egg-lifter and egg in mid-air and leant back against him briefly. Then the egg began to slide off the lifter and they both moved convulsively to save it and by a miracle it ended up on the plate, still sunny-side-up.

'That was a close shave,' he said into her ear.

'Yes. There's another frying to death in the pan. Can I . . .?'

'Nyree.' He turned her round to face him.

'What?' She tried to twist away.

'Can I look at you!' He wrested the egg-lifter out of her hand and put it down on the counter without taking his eyes off her face. 'What's wrong?' he said abruptly.

'Nothing! Look, just let me . . .'

'Forget about the egg. Do you think I don't know what's wrong?' he said curtly, his blue eyes no longer sleepy.

'It's not that,' she said defensively then bit her lip but decided to go on. 'This is the way I want it to be anyway. No strings, no . . . whatever. You have a conference to go to, I have a date with my boat. There is . . . just one thing. I'd rather Simon . . . didn't know.'

'Do you honestly think I'd do that?' he queried softly

but with a dangerous glint of anger in his eyes.

'I . . . no,' she answered, her shoulders slumping.

'Then do you honestly believe I'm—ready and willing to dash off anywhere? To . . . abandon you after what happened last night to all those morning-after-the-night-before doubts and fears I can see in your eyes.'

'I . . .' She licked her lips.

He waited. Then he said deliberately, 'You were sensational, Nyree.'

A wave of colour flooded her face.

'And now you're regretting it.'

'No,' she breathed. 'No, I couldn't, but . . .' She couldn't go on.

'But?' He pulled her closer and studied her hot face probingly until she averted it. 'But,' he said into her hair then, quietly, 'you find it hard to believe two people can affect each other like that? It even frightens you—for what it's worth, it sobers me. And on top of that you're tired, perhaps even sore—it's been a long time for you and it was hard not to get . . . carried away in the heat of the moment, for me.' He paused. 'Don't you think I can understand these things?' he asked then with a curious mixture of roughness and compassion.

She stood in the circle and shelter of his arms, washed by a feeling of supreme vulnerability, of sheer feminine helplessness, a feeling of needing his care and compassion now as much as she had gloried in his strength before. 'Oh Reid,' she whispered and laid her head on his shoulder. 'Sorry . . .'

'Don't—that's my line,' he said. 'I also know I'm

responsible for this state of affairs. Nyree . . .'

'Don't say it,' she warned and looked up with a trembling little smile.

He stared down into her eyes. 'You don't know what I was going to say.'

'And I don't want to. I'm . . . I can cope. Let's just take it as it comes. Please.' And her eyes were pleading, but calm now, and she stood up and kissed his lips.

An enormous spatter from the burning bacon in the pan made them both jump.

'Oh dear, I'll have to start again,' she said ruefully as they surveyed the pan.

CHAPTER SIX

HE LEFT her the following morning, early, and whatever he had been going to say remained unsaid.

Mainly, Nyree thought, because she'd had the sense—or from somewhere she'd found the strength—to relax and take it as it came. And to savour it without thinking ahead or back. It had been a unique day. He had persuaded her to go back to bed and they read the Sunday papers together although it was Monday, but they had both missed out on them the day before. And they had laughed at their black fingers and finger-marks on her white sheets then been too drowsy to do anything about it. And she had slept, deeply and dreamlessly for a couple of hours.

By which time the day had warmed up outside the warmth of the bedroom, and warmed the cockles of the Weather Bureau's heart by being perfect.

Nyree had woken up in his arms, feeling extraordinarily rested. And had said, 'Would you like to see my boat?'

They had spent the afternoon on the bay and it had been marvellous, just enough breeze to sail by, few boats about because it was a weekday, and then with a sunset almost equal to a Keppel special. Then they had hauled in the sail and used the motor to get back up-river between the green and red buoys. He had complimented her on her skills and she had complimented him on being a quick learner for a so-called novice. And the exhilaration had prompted them to shake hands gravely before stepping off on to the jetty, then him to pick her up and carry her off and hold her in a passionate embrace—to the delight of some passers-by.

'I didn't think that was possible,' she had said laughingly when he'd finally released her.

He had raised an eyebrow. 'That I'd want to kiss you?'

'No. I mean, yes, I do now but . . .' She had broken off, laughing again because she was getting tied up. 'What I meant was, I never thought . . . you know how you read about men sweeping women off their feet as if they were as light as feathers—I never thought it could happen to me. *That's* what I meant. What's so funny?' she had demanded with mock ire.

'Nothing,' he'd said, still grinning. 'But it's just as well I can sweep you off your feet.'

'Why?'

'It gives me a sense of security to know I'm at least stronger, even if you are miles ahead of me and I am an overgrown . . .'

'You don't believe that for a minute,' she'd retorted.

'That I'm stronger than you? Want to bet?' And he'd picked her up and carried her to the car.

'You know what I meant. You're just showing off now,' she had teased.

They had spent the evening quietly, watching some television then listening to music, and she had heated up some soup and some savoury crepes which they'd eaten in the lounge picnic style. Then they'd gone to bed and made love slowly and gently and it had been like another dimension to them. Not the mystery and fire of the previous night, not that searching, testing compulsion that had claimed them—and yes, she had had to acknowledge it had frightened her when she'd relived it in the cold light of day. No, it had been different, close and loving and caring. And she had slept in his arms afterwards.

There had been no misunderstandings over breakfast the next morning. She had cooked it very early while he'd showered, dressed in a dark suit, white shirt and maroon tie retrieved from the luggage he had in his car, and contacted the airline.

'Will there be any of the conference left?' she had asked lightly as she poured them coffee.

'Two days. Then I'm flying to Devonport in Tasmania but I'll be back in Brisbane by Friday. Simon goes back to school on Sunday night and I want to spend the weekend with him.'

'How is he? Is he with Amanda and Harold?'

'No. Didn't I tell you? He and Dean became inseparable over the last few days on Keppel and Jean suggested that Simon spend the week with them at home. They flew back on the same flight. I said she had more than enough to cope with but she seemed to think one more would be neither here nor there. And Simon was very keen. I thought, since it's the first time he appears to have made a close friend, it would be good for him—and I think the Porters genuinely wanted to have him. They live here in Brisbane at The Gap which is handy, because I'll be able to return the compliment on long weekends.'

'They were nice people, the Porters,' she had said sincerely.

'Mmm. What will you do?' he had asked directly.

'Take the boat out if the weather holds.'

He'd frowned. 'On your own?'

She'd smiled. 'Yesterday you were telling me what a skilful sailor I was,' she'd reminded him.

'I know but . . .'

'I'll be fine.' She had covered his hand briefly with her own then looked at her watch. 'It's getting late.'

'I guess so,' he had said reluctantly, then grimaced. 'I'm not terribly popular as it is. I forgot to cancel my reservation. This,' his blue eyes had sought her green ones, 'I guess this is the hard part. How to leave.' And he had captured her hand and drawn her down on to his lap.

She hadn't dressed, in fact she had only had time to put on a warm, fleecy sage-green robe and her hair was still loose although brushed. 'All right?' he had asked gently with one arm about her shoulders and his free hand fiddling with her hair, twisting it round and round his fingers.

'Fine,' she had said in a low voice but quite steadily. 'And you are—coming back?' That had slipped out unwittingly.

'Oh, yes—oh, yes.' He had kissed her lingeringly then parted the front of her robe and touched her breasts, cupping them in turn and stroking her nipples. 'You're so beautiful. Take care on that boat, won't you?' he had said huskily.

'I will . . .'

'I don't think I can go.'

'You can—but not if you keep doing that.'

'You're right.' He had grinned and closed her robe up to her throat. 'While not the most important conference, I guess I should be there. Do you know what a nuisance bots are?'

'Bots? I've never heard of them. What are they?'

'Well, there's this cunning fly, the gadfly, that lays its eggs on horses mainly, where they can lick at them and—I won't bore you with all the details—but gradually ingest them to the stomach where they become full-blown parasitic larvae known as bots.'

'It sounds horrible!'

'It can be very debilitating and even fatal. But Matthews & Inchwood are right there in the forefront to combat them.'

'I feel as if I'm sending you off to a war,' she had said, and they had laughed together softly. And the moment had been breached, coped with and solved.

But after their last embrace and when the door had closed on him, she had thought, that's the way to do it. Lightly and with humour . . .

'Only,' she had murmured aloud, 'I've done the unthinkable, haven't I? Have I . . . become a mistress—again? Will it be like this whenever he's away, will I doubt what I've done and be scared of the day . . . the day when he leaves me? What was he going to say yesterday morning? Practically speaking, if he ever did find that he'd like to provide Simon with a stepmother, well, at least he knows how well we get on. But that would be a hollow victory . . .'

Later in the day, she managed to quash her qualms,

to persuade herself to take her own advice, to persist in the knowledge that she loved him and nothing could change it, but to take it one day at a time.

She locked up her flat and went sailing.

He came back as he'd promised. In fact she found him on her doorstep several days later when she got home from the first day of the term—the night after Simon would have gone back to school.

'Reid! Have you been waiting long?'

'About seventy-two hours, twenty-five minutes too long,' he said gravely. 'I came on the off-chance that you'd be home about now.'

'You could have called . . .'

'I couldn't wait another moment. Are you going to ask me in?'

'Of course.'

'Knowing full well what I have in mind?' His blue eyes glinted with devilry.

'Oh, I generally have a cup of tea at this time of the afternoon, too,' she said demurely and put her key in the lock.

That was four o'clock roughly but it wasn't until well after six that she got her tea.

He didn't stay the night, though, and it was four days before she saw him again, and once again he surprised her by simply turning up on her doorstep.

She pondered this lack of forward planning—for want of a better description—but couldn't convince herself that it was aimed at keeping her on a string. Because subsequently he missed her a couple of times, and slipped outrageous notes under her door . . . *Nyree,*

What does that mean anyway? Is it Maori or Maltic—I mean Maltese? Whatever, I missed you multitudinously and your missish neighbour is making me uncomfortable. I'm off to wage mayhem on march flies which drive most mammals to marginal madness. Did you say make love not war? Signed, Matthews. R.

And . . . *Hell, she's peering out of her bathroom window again—she must have some sixth sense. Couldn't you tell her I'm the man who comes to dinner or a long lost cousin or that your television has bots? Warm regards and I'm off to have a cold shower. Reid—oh that guy, what was his second name?*

'I think I might have to give you a key,' Nyree said judiciously, the next time he came.

'Oh? Why?'

'You've got my next-door neighbour, who is a maiden lady and extremely inquisitive, into a twitter.'

'Ah-ha! But if she's a maiden lady won't that get her into more of a twitter?'

'No. You see what alerts her is your knocking several times on the door and then when you hang about writing me epistles, well that really excites her. Whereas if you could just let yourself in, she mightn't even know, let alone come in to have long, probing chats with me.'

He laughed but accepted the key gravely. 'Sure?'

'Sure.'

She came to the conclusion that this was a better way of doing things for them both. His life was obviously spent very much on the move and he had made it clear he didn't expect her to wait around for him. It also occurred to her that it was important not to project the image of someone pining for him, that he could feel pressurised or threatened—nor was it good for her to be sitting around languishing between visits.

Accordingly, she joined a theatre club and took up golf. And it was only when she was tired and lonely, and Reid was on the other side of the continent or, for all she knew, at home in Brisbane, that she sometimes questioned her plan and wondered if she was doing the right thing. Not only that, whether she wasn't taking out subtle insurance against the day when he would leave her. Yet it comforted her, she found, to think that nobody knew, not even Miss Hambro, who might suspect but didn't, she was sure, have the range of experience to imagine what passionate lovers she and Reid had become. And that was the way she wanted it to stay.

Curiously, it was about this that they came close to an argument during those two months. And fatefully but indirectly, it was the key to the flat she gave him that ended their affair—once again the hand of fate chose to remain hidden, she was to think afterwards.

But in the meantime their near-argument came out of the blue.

It was a wet Saturday afternoon and the game of golf she had planned had been called off, and she had decided to spend the time correcting essays. But Reid arrived and they spent the afternoon in bed mostly, in a quiet way.

He looked weary, she thought, and as if he had something on his mind. And she started to ask him about it then changed her mind, and instead, she took the initiative in bed, but slowly and gently as if to restore him with her hands and body and lips.

Finally his body shuddered in release above hers, in her arms, and she held him tightly until he was still at last.

'Nyree?' he said some time later, raising himself on one elbow.

She opened her eyes and stared into his blue ones. 'Mmm?'

'That was all very well for me, in fact it was . . .' He stopped and kissed her forehead. 'But for you . . .'

'It's all right,' she murmured, and put a finger on his lips. 'It doesn't have to happen every time for me.'

'No?' He bit her fingertip gently.

'No.' She stirred beneath his weight. 'Sometimes it can be for—well, comfort and consolation, can't it? And that gives me another kind of pleasure, I guess.'

'It's not,' he stopped and frowned faintly, 'it's not that way for men, generally. And how did you know?'

'You looked tired,' she said simply. 'And men and women are different. But don't worry, next time I might leap on you and wrestle you to the floor as soon as you get in the door.'

His body jolted with laughter and he kissed her then rolled away, but taking her with him so that they were lying facing each other. 'Thanks,' he said softly. 'I was tired but now I feel like a million quid. Know what I'd like to do? I'd like to wine, dine and dance you tonight. Shall we?'

'It's pouring.'

'Don't you own an umbrella? Not that I'd expect you to walk anyway.'

She was silent.

He sat up abruptly and said in a different voice, 'Nyree, there's no earthly reason why we shouldn't be seen together. There's only one person we're hiding this state of affairs from, and Simon would be the last person to see us.'

'I . . .' she said hesitantly, 'all right. If that's what you want.'

'No, it's not what I want,' he said irritably. 'At least not to feel as if I'm dragging you out against your better judgement. Forget it,' he added brusquely, and turned away.

She stared at the long, strong lines of his back and wondered at her reluctance. Was it a lack of faith? Did she want to keep their relationship from the whole world so that no one could look upon her with pity if it ended?

She reached out tentatively and stroked his back, thinking, if . . . when . . . no, strike those words out.

Her hand left his back and she sat up behind him with a sort of twisted grace, her legs drawn up beside her, and she said in a low voice, 'Sorry. I was being silly. I've . . . actually I've got a new dress and depending on where you want to go, perhaps I could christen it.'

She thought that he wasn't going to respond so that when he turned back slowly at last, her eyes were wary. And he said nothing but raised a knee and rested his elbow on it and his head on his wrist. And his gaze travelled up and down her body, lingering on her thighs, her breasts and the jutting curve of her hip. She had all but lost her tan from Keppel and her skin was pale but satiny, almost translucent in the blueish light of the storm-laden afternoon, pale and naked and vulnerable, whereas he was still deeply tanned.

And that was how she felt beneath his scrutiny, as she sat within his reach, straight-backed and with her uncertainty showing in her eyes. And her fingers suddenly reaching for and gripping the sheet to cover herself, to escape that enigmatic gaze.

'Don't,' he said, raising his head and dropping his arm unhurriedly to entwine his fingers with hers on the sheet. 'You don't have to.'

She went to look away but his hand left hers and cupped her cheek then slid around the back of the slender column of her neck to draw her forward gently as he had done once before until their foreheads touched.

And he said very quietly, 'You know, I could make love to you again, right now. But I think you'd better show me this dress, because there's *no* reason to be afraid of coming out to dinner with me, but if you don't, that's what will happen. Only, that way, I could end up an old man before my time.'

She closed her eyes and her heart felt like bursting with relief. 'You're,' her lips trembled into a smile, 'you're crazy, you know,' she said huskily.

'Is it in aid of something special, this peach of a dress?' he enquired over dinner.

The restaurant was dim, but warm and elegant with the sheen of polished silver and glassware, and fragrant with bowls of creamy rosebuds on the tables.

Nyree looked down at her new dress, best described

as a cocktail dress probably, and in an unusual shade of shimmering, silvery pewter. It was a tissuey material, and in the elbow-length puffed sleeves it was narrowly pleated, whereas the low-waist bodice with a square neckline was smooth. And the narrow pleats were repeated in the skirt beneath a self sash. She wore pale grey stockings and her grey kid shoes, and a long string of lustrous cultured pearls that had been her father's eighteenth birthday present to her. Her hair was up but loosely as she had only recently begun to wear it, and the wet weather had induced the wisps that had escaped to curve.

Reid had arrived at the flat in a charcoal suit and a blue shirt, and in them again she thought he looked almost terrifyingly handsome.

'Thanks,' she said warmly. 'It's in aid of the school formal. The senior year's coming-out dance.'

'Isn't it a bit early for that?'

'Well, it's not for a few weeks but they like to get it out of the way before that last burst of study and the exams. I just happened to see the dress and thought— ah, that solves that problem!' she said whimsically.

He smiled slightly. 'You could be the belle of the ball.'

'Thank you again but not really,' she said wryly. 'The girls they invite, most of them, wear what could only be described as ball gowns. Strapless and backless, yards of skirt, gloves, ribbons etcetera, . . . why are you looking at me like that?'

He raised an eyebrow. 'I was enjoying the contrast.'

She stared at him, puzzled.

He said idly, 'I was imagining you in something

strapless and backless and thinking how glad I was that you weren't.'

'I don't . . .'

'I know you don't flaunt yourself if that's what you were going to say. Which is just as well because it might be a sore test of my self-control—most men's, perhaps. But also, I wouldn't have the pleasure of seeing you now, looking lovely and elegant but cool and reserved and refined—and then thinking of how you look in bed. Gorgeous—and like a Goddess of Love. Although,' he studied her critically, 'not quite so cool as . . .'

'Are you surprised,' she broke in, putting her hands to her warm cheeks. 'I thought we'd come out to . . . to . . .'

'We did.' His lips twisted and a glint of blue devilry played over her. 'And you're right—we should change the subject before this gets out of hand. What were we talking about? Oh yes. That unnerving event when you're at that age—your senior high dance.'

'I don't believe you found yours unnerving,' she said ruefully.

'I did. I invited this exquisite, gossamer-like creature I'd had my eye on for months but she was so shy we hardly talked, and I—well, kept tripping over my own feet. I've improved since those days,' he said gravely.

'I don't believe a word of that,' she retorted. 'I'm sure you were *born* charming females.'

He laughed. 'Don't you believe it. What about the staff?'

'What about them?'

'Do they take partners?'

'You can if you want to but most don't. I won't.'

He sat forward, all amusement suddenly drained from his expression. 'Do you really enjoy teaching, Nyree?'

She hesitated. 'I find it both frustrating and rewarding. I think,' she paused, 'most teachers often grapple with not so much teaching as motivating children to want to learn.'

'And the milieu? I mean you went straight from university to teaching, didn't you? You must enjoy the academic life-style.'

'I do,' she said honestly. 'But I think you can take a—well, a reasonably academic view of life wherever. I mean even if you are isolated from the ... the institutions you can still read and study if you want to, can't you? And I do sometimes think that in schools and universities, the atmosphere becomes too rarefied sometimes.'

He absorbed all she had said with a curious intentness and she was just beginning to feel curious herself when he smiled and changed the subject totally. 'Would you care to dance, Miss Westbrook? We never have, you know.'

'Is that a good idea?' she asked, her lips curving and with an imp of mischief in her eyes.

'Definitely not so cool as on Keppel,' he drawled. 'But I think it's a great idea.'

The dance-floor was small and fairly crowded. At first Nyree felt awkward and conspicuous—they were the tallest couple on the floor. And Reid looked at her with an eyebrow raised.

'I haven't done much dancing for years,' she apologised.

'This isn't really dancing,' he commented, drawing her closer. 'This is more being together to music. Relax.'

In fact the beat was slow and the music dreamy, and after a time she began to lose herself in it—and in him. And when the band took a break, she woke up as if from a dream, smiled at him a little dazedly and murmured, 'You have improved.'

He laughed and kissed her forehead.

They left soon afterwards, hand in hand, and didn't speak until they were on her doorstep. Then she looked at him enquiringly, waking up a bit from the spell of togetherness that had her in its grip.

He said, 'I wasn't going to stay the night. I—Simon has the day off tomorrow, but . . .'

'I'll make you a cup of coffee then,' she interrupted.

They drank their coffee side by side on the settee with some soft music playing and only the lamp above the dining-table on.

'Nyree,' he said, putting his cup down and drawing her against his shoulder, 'why don't you come out with us tomorrow? Simon still talks about you and . . .'

'No,' she whispered, fingering the lapel of his jacket, smoothing it, raising it up and smoothing it again. Then she curled her feet under her and tilted her face up to him. 'Tell me . . . tell me something about your life-style, Reid. Are you happy with it?'

It was of course, she realised, a bid to change the subject but the irony of it was not to hit her until later.

Nor was she to wonder until later why it was such a successful bid.

But his eyes narrowed and he frowned. 'Why do you ask that?'

Why had she? It had just—come to mind, although hadn't he asked her something similar earlier? 'I—I thought you looked tired and,' she shrugged slightly, 'tense when you arrived. I told you.'

He leant his head back against the cushion. 'We are contemplating some changes in the firm which will mean I won't be spending half my life in aircraft, commercial ones or the company plane.'

'Do you—are you a pilot?'

'Yes. Didn't you know?'

'No.'

'Well, I was always interested in flying—a lot of outback properties these days have their own planes and airstrips and the one we lived on had a fleet virtually. So I got my pilot's licence before I qualified and it's come in very handy . . .'

'The flying vet,' she said softly.

'Mmm. I also have a licence to fly helicopters. But lately it's become . . .' He stopped and they both sat up. 'What the hell was that?'

'I don't know . . . next-door I . . .' Nyree stopped mid-sentence as a series of muffled bangs and squeaks made themselves heard from the flat next door. Then there was a final crash like a door being slammed almost off its hinges, and a moment later someone was pounding on her door.

It was Miss Hambro, looking wild and distraught in a long flannel nightgown and with her wispy grey hair confined beneath a net. 'Oh, thank God,' she sobbed as Nyree opened her door and she all but fell through it. 'I didn't know if you'd be home! I didn't know what to do—oh, it was awful!' And she fell into Nyree's arms.

Nyree frowned across the top of her head at Reid then said to the shaking figure in her arms, 'It's all right, you're safe now. There, there . . . Miss Hambro. You're quite safe now,' she said gently. 'Look, come in and sit down and tell us about it. Was it a burglar?'

'No!' It came out as a muffled wail. 'Worse! I can cope with burglars, I can cope with a lot of things but . . .' Miss Hambro disengaged herself and drew herself up to her full height, which was about five foot two. 'I'd like to see any burglar get into my flat!' she said scornfully.

'Then . . .?'

Miss Hambro slumped. 'It was a mouse,' she said hollowly. 'I can't abide mice. When I was a child I lived through a plague of mice up on the Downs. You couldn't open a drawer or a cupboard without them jumping out at you . . . ugh!' She shuddered then drew a deep quivering breath. 'I must have been asleep, you see, Nyree. Yes. But I don't sleep very much these days and I keep a little snack on my bedside table too, so that when I wake up I, well, I don't have to just lie there, I suppose. Anyway, I woke up and would you believe it, there was this mouse nibbling at my snack! Yes. And straightway I was transported back—good Lord—about sixty *years*. I could see them again, nasty furry creatures, rivers of them. I . . . I think I panicked,' she said ingenuously and blinked several times at Nyree. 'Yes. How stupid . . .'

But Nyree was laughing and she hugged Miss Hambro again. 'You poor thing. I can just imagine how you felt! Look, I'm going to make you a cup of tea while we work out how to deal with this mouse. By the way, I don't think I've introduced you to my . . . guest. Miss Hambro, this is Reid Matthews. I'm sure he'll . . . know how to handle a mouse.'

'Oh!' Miss Hambro turned convulsively, her eyes all but popping. 'I didn't realise you weren't alone. Oh, dear me—how do you do—I didn't mean, oh, look at me . . .' She petered out looking pink and flustered and clutching first at her hairnet and then her nightgown, then her eyes widened in obvious recognition and she looked even more embarrassed and flustered.

But Reid was superb. He shook her hand gravely, told her he was a vet and that he was much interested in the mice-plague phenomenon—wasn't it strange how they came out of the blue and then disappeared sometimes equally abruptly? And what year and what part of the Downs was it because it was interesting to compare . . .

And within a few minutes, Miss Hambro was sitting down comfortably and regaling him with the details while Nyree made the tea. And it was half an hour before he said that perhaps he ought to go and investigate this impudent mouse.

That was when Miss Hambro tumbled back to earth from her eager reminiscences, struck the side of her wrinkled face with her palm and said, 'Oh, no. Oh, dear!'

'What is it?' Nyree asked.

'I've locked myself out! I banged the door shut as hard as I could but the lock would have been on the latch. It's a deadlock. Oh dear!'

'Perhaps I can find a way to get in,' Reid said soothingly.

'I just don't think that's possible,' Miss Hambro said sadly.

'She's right,' Reid said to Nyree some time later in the kitchen. 'The place is as impregnable as Boggo Road unless I break a window. Heaven knows how the poor mouse got in.'

They laughed together quietly. Then Nyree said, 'I'll have to ask her to stay the night.'

'Isn't it lucky we hadn't gone to bed? I should have damaged your reputation for ever. I'll go now.' He kissed her gently, hesitated then said, 'I don't know when—I'm off up-country on Monday . . .'

'It doesn't matter. I'll be here,' she said, leaning against him briefly.

'Well, not only is he the best-looking man I've seen for years but so nice, Nyree!' Miss Hambro said when Reid had left. 'Only I feel a little . . .' She broke off and bit her lip.

'It's all right, he was going anyway,' Nyree said serenely, but at the same time thanking heaven she had made the bed up freshly before she and Reid had gone out to dinner. 'Now I'm going to make up the settee for me and you can have my bed. No, no arguments,' she said to the old lady. 'You see, I've slept here before when my aunt has visited me.'

'Ah! Yes, I remember last year, wasn't it? You had a

visitor for several days. An,' she groped for words, 'an unusual looking lady, um . . .'

'That would be my aunt,' Nyree agreed. 'She always looks as if she's going for a cross-country hike. She spends a lot of time in the bush observing animals and dresses in the expectation that she might have to whizz over to Tasmania to verify a sighting of the Tasmanian Tiger. In fact she's over there now. Has been for the last three months.' And how relieved I am that she is, she'll never know, Nyree thought, thinking of her aunt for the first time for ages—and recalling how upset that lady had become over her entanglement with Brad. She came back to the present. 'I'll just get changed first. Like a second cuppa?' she asked.

'Oh, no. You've been so kind as it is. I feel . . .' Miss Hambro blinked away a tear and Nyree patted her hand affectionately.

It was only much later, in the dark and when she was trying to get comfortable on the settee, that Nyree thought back to her conversation with Reid—and she finally fell asleep with a curious question mark on her mind.

CHAPTER SEVEN

A WEEK passed with no word from Reid.

Then he rang her to say that he would be away for at least another week, but wherever he was ringing from remained a secret, because the line kept fading and crackling and they finally gave up trying to make themselves further understood. But she felt warmed because it was the first time he had done that. And she wondered if she should have gone out with him and Simon—she would have loved to have seen Simon, everything else aside.

In the meantime the school formal drew closer and then the night was upon her, but when she was ready to leave her car refused to start. She cursed it soundly and called for a taxi, which took some time to come with the net result that she arrived late and breathless. This earned her a reproachful look from the deputy headmaster but a burst of applause from the boys.

As she slipped into her place at the staff table she was not only breathless but fairly pink.

'Wow!' Peter Marshall, the rather trendy music master, said into her ear, 'you look marvellous, my dear Nyree!'

'Thanks,' she said out of the side of her mouth. 'I *feel* horribly conspicuous, not to mention hot and bothered—my car wouldn't start. How's it going?'

'Too early to say. It's generally after dinner that couples tend to disappear into the shrubbery and the

146

punch suddenly and mysteriously livens up.'

They grinned at each other, then the first course was served in the gaily decorated, towering stone refectory, but Peter Marshall's gaze lingered on her.

Later he asked her to dance twice, which she did unaffectedly. He said, after the second dance, 'We've known each other for several years now, haven't we, Nyree?'

'Have we? Yes, I guess we have. Time flies.'

He smiled faintly. 'But it's only very lately that I've thought you looked . . . different. Want to tell me about it?'

She was caught off guard. 'Do I?'

'Yes. Less efficient, more human.'

She grimaced then said lightly, 'It must be spring.'

And the headmaster himself came up and with old fashioned courtesy asked her to dance. They circled the floor to the appreciation of everyone. He said, 'Nyree—may I call you that? I count your aunt as a great friend of mine.'

Nyree blinked. 'Of course, but I didn't know . . . I mean I knew you knew my aunt but . . .'

He permitted himself a small smile. 'She's a true eccentric. But I wanted to compliment you, my dear. You have the makings of a very good teacher. Your senior English class this year promises excellent results and I think this last semester has been the turning-point for them. You've taught from the heart. I just hope,' he looked at her searchingly, 'you recognise your true vocation with us.'

'I . . . I'm not planning to leave or anything,' Nyree said dazedly, feeling there was something more behind this speech than she could put her finger on.

'Good.' He smiled then reverted to his normal brisk, practical manner. 'There's a young lady over there rather the worse for wear, I suspect. Would you mind assisting her?'

So it was a mixed evening for Nyree and one she would never forget. A proud evening, and not only because of the unexpected praise from the headmaster, but because all her students, looking so different and grown-up in their dinner suits, brought their partners over to be introduced as if they really wanted her to meet them.

But there was a puzzling aspect to it as well. And she thought once with a sudden pang—I'm obviously different and people can see it. Do they know I'm in *love*? If they do—does Reid?

Mostly, however, it was the most enjoyable school formal she had attended.

Peter Marshall offered her a lift home which she accepted gratefully. A capricious spring storm had sprung up and was drenching Brisbane. And, possibly spurred on by her successes of the evening, she invited him up for coffee.

He had always been friendly but in a disinterested manner. She knew he was unmarried but with a taste for rather exotic women, that he travelled extensively in the holidays, that he was passionate about Gustav Mahler and playing the cello—and viewed the rest of life with a wry sense of humour.

That he was viewing her with less detachment was obvious as they chatted about and laughed over the evening and some of their teaching experiences. But it never occurred to her that she had awoken any intimate interest in him.

Then she got up to pour them more coffee and was handing his cup to him and smiling at something he was saying when she was gripped by a queer intuition. She turned her head towards the hall doorway.

Reid was standing there in the shadows.

She gasped, blinked and straightened with the cup still in her hand. 'Reid! I didn't hear . . .' She trailed off as he moved and the light fell on his face. And her eyes widened at the blaze of anger in his blue eyes, the harsh lines beside his mouth. And her mouth fell open as he spoke.

He said with unmistakable menace, 'Who the hell is this?'

There was an unnatural silence for a few moments.

Then Peter Marshall stood up and his gaze wandered from Nyree's stunned face to the keys Reid still held in his hand, and he said finally, 'Well, forgive me if I'm poaching on forbidden territory, but I didn't know. You might have warned me, Nyree,' he added ruefully. 'But don't let me be the cause of any disruption.' He looked back at Reid and said levelly, 'This is quite innocent, mate.'

And he walked out with a last wry gaze at Nyree, studiously ignoring Reid.

They heard the front door close and Nyree came to life. 'How *dare* you!' she spat at Reid.

'What did you expect me to do?' he retorted. 'Join the queue?'

'You . . .' She had trouble speaking. 'There is no *queue* and I don't have to be insulted by anyone, least of all you. You don't own me and I'll invite who I like up here . . .'

'And sleep with whoever you like?' he broke in grimly.

She closed her eyes briefly and felt like fainting from sheer rage. 'There was never any *intention* . . .'

'Wasn't there, Nyree?' He looked at her sardonically. 'I was watching him and I can tell you it wasn't the furthest thing from his mind. Who the hell is he anyway?'

She took a steadying breath and said arctically, 'A fellow teacher.'

'Of course—it was the school dance.' He moved forward into the lounge until he was right in front of her, and looked her up and down thoughtfully, at the silvery dress and the pink carnation tucked into her hair which she had forgotten about and had had pressed on her by one of her students. 'Quite a night by the look of things,' he murmured, his blue eyes still hard. 'I thought you said you wouldn't be taking a partner? It obviously didn't occur to you to invite me.'

Nyree suddenly realised she was still clutching a full cup of coffee. She put it down carefully and said very carefully, 'I did not take a partner. My car wouldn't start so I took a taxi there—Peter offered me a lift home, it was pouring. And I didn't have the faintest idea where you were so how could I have asked you?'

'We could have made a long range . . . date. But that isn't part of your plan, is it, Nyree?'

She stared at him and it was like looking at a stranger, a tall, grim-faced stranger. She said, 'I don't know what you mean. But I do know you've humiliated me, you seem to think you can turn up here as if you own the place, you think you can pass ridiculous judgements on me, you, you . . .'

'I don't think anything of the kind,' he said coldly. 'You were the one who gave me a key and urged me to use it rather than exciting Miss Hambro, you assured me you'd be here although I didn't know when I would be back. As for ridiculous judgements there is only this, I believe in being exclusive inside or outside marriage, so if you want to play the field . . .'

'Marriage!' she flashed at him. 'I don't know how you've got the nerve to mention the word! As for parading your pompous,' she gritted her teeth, 'morals at me when for all I know you're sleeping with women from Darwin to . . . to Devonport . . .'

'I'm not.' His eyes glinted with anger again and his lips set in a hard line.

'But how do I *know* that?' she asked scornfully. 'How am I to know anything?' She stopped suddenly, realising she was baring more of her soul than she should, baring all her latent fears and, yes, secret despair.

But then she thought, that aside, there's a principle at stake, isn't there? And she wiped her mouth with the back of her hand because she was close to tears but determined to fight.

'You have a secretary, don't you? You meet women in the course of your affairs, your business affairs?' she said with irony. 'Should I wonder if you're sleeping with them because you happen to have a cup of coffee with them?'

'At half past midnight and with someone . . . devouring me with their eyes, you'd be entitled to wonder,' he said with equal irony.

'He wasn't,' she whispered.

'He was. Didn't you hear what he said about

encroaching on forbidden territory? What other reason would he have for saying that?'

'Then *I* wasn't . . .'

'You looked as if you were lapping it up,' he said shortly, and with a gesture that surprised her, he reached out and removed the flower from her hair. 'Did he give you this?'

'No. Reid . . .' She was white to the lips and shaking inwardly. 'I think you'd better go. If you can't trust me, if you think those things of me . . . anyway, it had to end some time, didn't it?'

Their eyes clashed. 'Do you want it to end?' he asked abruptly.

'Yes,' she heard herself say and tried to blink away a haze of tears at the same time as she felt as if she were plunging a knife into her own heart. But it was that sensation of pain that stiffened her resolve and tore the veils from her mind . . . Oh, I thought I was coping so well, she marvelled. I thought I could heal him and change him, but the plain truth is the longer it lasts the worse the wounds will be for *me*, because I *can't* change him. I can only love him and hate him but I can't change him.

She turned away, then turned back with the tears checked although her lips were trembling. But her voice was surprisingly steady as she said, 'Yes.'

'I wondered about that,' he said quietly, his eyes unreadable but with a nerve beating in his jaw. 'You've been very careful to make no claims. You've also . . . blossomed like a flower.' He looked down at the pink bloom in his hands. 'But the two things don't go together. Have I been like an exorcist for you, Nyree?' He looked up and straight across into her green eyes.

'Yes,' she said simply. 'I didn't . . . start out thinking that but that's the way it's happened. I don't really know how or why. I can only thank you and . . . hope you understand. Perhaps I lost confidence in myself after Brad. You've restored it.'

She stopped speaking and wondered how it was possible to lie so calmly. She wondered if he would guess that something was bleeding to death inside her. She wondered why he looked unusually pale but guessed he was angry.

'So,' he said at last, 'that's that.'

'I'm sorry,' she whispered.

'So am I. We were good together, rather well matched, I thought, my Amazon.'

She closed her eyes.

'Oh, I wasn't trying to insult you,' he said softly, and touched the point of her chin with his knuckles. 'Just . . . bidding you farewell.'

She tried to speak but couldn't.

He watched her for a long moment, almost as if committing her face to memory, but that couldn't be, she knew. If anything, he would want to forget it.

Then he walked out, stopping only to lay the flower and her key on the dining-table.

She slept that night because she was too numbed and exhausted to do anything else.

But the next morning, Saturday fortunately, she had not the heart even to get dressed. Instead, the day passed in a blur. And Sunday started out the same way, a day of misery and pain, a day of castigating herself for not understanding how she had fooled herself. How she had allowed her hopes to build up. How she had hoped, by accepting that he was wary and disbelieving, by making no claims, forging no ties that he would come to believe in her and her love. Only to have the opposite happen . . . And perhaps that hurt most of all, she thought. He hadn't realised what the change in her was all about. He had wondered about it and come to the conclusion that he had been instrumental in helping her to shed the shackles of the past, that was all. No . . . that she was now *receptive* to the advances of other men. It really didn't bear thinking about but think about it she did, round and round.

At about midday, she realised her doorbell was ringing and that it had rung and the door had been knocked upon twice, earlier.

She sighed, looked down at herself in her sage-green robe, and went to answer it.

Miss Hambro stood there quivering with distress.

'Oh,' Nyree said vaguely. 'Has the mouse come back? I thought the pest control man . . .'

'My dear, my dear child,' Miss Hambro broke in, 'don't take on so. Life has to go on, you know. Now let me in because it's not good for you to be so alone.'

Nyree blinked but didn't bother to dissemble. 'You know? How?'

'I got up on Friday night—Saturday morning really—it was well after midnight, because I've been having more trouble sleeping than usual lately, since the mouse,' she said humourlessly, 'and I went into the kitchen to boil the kettle. Well, as you know our kitchen windows look out on the corridor, and the corridor light happens to be above my window . . . and I saw Mr Matthews leaving. I saw his face quite clearly. It was—not hard to tell from his expression that something had gone wrong. But I waited all day yesterday for some sign of you. Then when you wouldn't even answer the door this morning, I knew I was right.'

Nyree smiled painfully. 'You were,' she said quietly. 'It's ... finished between us,' she stopped and leant against the wall tiredly, 'and I can't believe I could have been such a fool, not me ...' And to her dismay, the tears she had held back for a day and a half started to flow.

To say that Miss Hambro took charge with delight would have been wrong. But she certainly did so with loving efficiency. She stayed with Nyree for the rest of the day, alternately cosseting her with kindness and offering her gems of wisdom. She washed the dishes and cleaned up the kitchen which Nyree had neglected since Friday night, she put a load of washing through the washing-machine. She dusted and swept and tidied up and made them an evening meal. She even offered to stay the night, but by that time Nyree had taken hold ...

'You've been so kind,' she said softly, taking both the old lady's hands in hers. 'I don't know what I would have done without you. But I'll be all right now. As you said, life has to go on, and I've had my period of mourning if that's what you should call it. Thank you.'

'Is there,' Miss Hambro blinked away a sudden tear, 'is there no hope? He seemed such a nice man ... I mean ...' She trailed off awkwardly.

'He is,' Nyree said. 'But no, not for us.'

It was less hard than she had expected the next day to face Peter Marshall. Which she had decided she must do at the first opportunity.

But he forestalled her when they met in the staff-room and she walked up to him determinedly. 'Nyree, don't look so serious,' he said lightly. 'It was just one of life's little encounters.'

'It wasn't and I feel I owe you an explanation and an apology,' she said quietly. 'Only,' she bit her lip, 'I don't quite know where to begin.'

'Look,' he said, 'you don't have to. I've had a chance to think about it over the weekend and once my natural,' he grinned faintly, 'indignation subsided I . . . er . . . recalled that men in love behave peculiarly sometimes. I know I have . . .'

'He . . .' Nyree interrupted but Peter disregarded her.

'I also remembered that I'd speculated upon whether something like this had happened to you and thus,' he said wryly, 'I can't complain at being proved right. But by the same token, I can't deny that I . . . wish it were otherwise, or to put it another way, that I was the man who'd made you . . . glow as you did.'

Nyree winced for several reasons—one being that in her heart she had still wanted Reid to have been wrong about Peter. But it seemed he had not been.

'You're very . . . I don't know what to say,' she murmured.

'You don't have to say anything. But if this relationship does prove to be a flash in the pan, well, I'll be around.'

All through that long, long day, Nyree wondered whether Peter would ever know the irony of it all.

But if her teaching day was long and arduous with

the strain of not looking as she felt, there was no respite when she got home. Her aunt was waiting on her doorstep.

Yet, a week later, when her aunt had left to pursue a rare species of possum, she felt as if it might have been the best thing for her. Because, with the memory unexpectedly sharp and clear in her mind of the bitter denunciation she had endured of herself and Brad last time around, there was no way she was going to endure it again. She even warned Miss Hambro, who was becoming like a member of the family, not to mention Reid.

Which was not to say she wasn't fond of her mother's sister, but how to explain to someone who saw things in either black or white that she had lost out on love again? For that matter it was hard enough to explain to herself, but with an iron will she hadn't known she possessed she allowed none of her confusion, her pain and bitterness or anger and despair to show—her aunt even complimented her fondly at the end of her stay on how well she was managing her life.

'I think we're a lot alike, you know,' she said by way of a parting shot. 'Able to dedicate ourselves.' Her eyes, the same colour as Nyree's, glowed with enthusiasm.

Nyree forbore to comment but sent her off to the possum hunt with fond but inwardly intensely relieved farewells.

As the weeks slipped by and the weather became warm and humid, she gave thanks for her aunt's visit, because after that intense effort of will, the habit had become ingrained.

Or so she thought until one evening when she looked through a drawer and came upon Reid's notes.

She immediately forgot what she had been looking for as she read them again, and the pain of losing him sliced through her, taking her breath away. But what surprised her was how the memories came crowding back when she had thought she had them so firmly at bay. And she realised dimly that she had only achieved it by directing a lot of her anger and bitterness at Reid.

Well, who wouldn't? she mused. He had been unforgivable that last night . . .

But the fact remained that now, on a hot November night, sitting at her desk correcting exam papers for her Grade Elevens—at least that's what she had been doing—she was instead sitting with her head in her hands and with all the wonderful memories of Reid flooding her mind, and the bitterness seeping away . . . Not the sadness, no, she thought, nor the pain, but I can't seem to be angry with him any more. I can only remember . . . oh, God!

She put her knuckles to her mouth and closed her eyes as she saw him so clearly in her mind's eye and remembered his strength and his gentleness, how they had made love with sometimes wild abandon, sometimes laughing tenderness. She recalled Great Keppel and Simon, a little boy lost in a welter of adult emotions, a child who had touched her heart.

'It would have . . . it could have worked,' she whispered to herself in anguish. 'I could have made it work if only you'd let me . . . Where are you now, I wonder? With someone new? Someone you'll never make the mistake of letting get too close ... Did I come too close to the forbidden territory of your heart? It might help me to think that, but I'll never really know. I can only hope ... that you're at peace, because I love you and I can never change. You see, I even have a basis for reference—if I thought I was hurt before, it was nothing to this. I was a naïve innocent with Brad but with you ... with you, you're like a part of me ...'

The exams came and went, December arrived and finally break-up day.

It was that evening that she realised the long Christmas holidays had crept up on her unnoticed. She had no plans and could think of none. All she could acknowledge was that she was weary and drained.

So that when the phone rang she answered it listlessly.

'Nyree? Is that you? Gwen Foster here.'

CHAPTER EIGHT

'GWEN! This is a pleasant surprise,' Nyree said into the phone. 'You must have been wondering if I'd left town, I guess. I should have rung.'

'Well, I was a little concerned,' Gwen confessed, 'but you did say you wanted a break and I know what a busy time of the year this is for teachers. How are you, my dear?'

'Fine,' Nyree said brightly, assuming her public role. 'Did you . . . did you have something in mind for me?' she added cautiously, thinking suddenly—this is where it all began . . .

'I have to be honest, yes,' Gwen said ruefully. 'But I won't press you—it's just a rush job that's come up and, well, you know what the holidays are like—I'm always stretched to the limit at this time of the year.'

'Gwen, I'm really rather tired . . .'

'Well, it's only an overnight job, Nyree,' Gwen interrupted. 'Let me give you some details and then you can decide.' Nyree took the phone from her ear and grimaced at it. 'The husband has been unexpectedly asked to attend a conference overseas and the wife has been invited too. Now they have three children aged five, three and six months and it's been arranged for the children to spend the time with their grandparents who live in Central Queensland, on a cattle property. And because this has come up at such

160

short notice, they've arranged to fly the children up on a private plane but they need someone to accompany them. So you'd fly up on Sunday, hand the children over and return on Monday. How does that sound?'

Nyree hesitated. 'Couldn't they put them on a commercial flight?'

'There are no commercial flights—there are no towns within reasonable range, you know, without the grandparents having to drive hundreds of miles, but there is an airstrip on the property or to be precise, the neighbouring one, and it's really the simplest way to get the children up there. In fact anything they need in a hurry goes up that way.'

'So where will I spend the night?'

'On, let me see,' Gwen said, 'Niranda Downs station. It's a very large property and they have a guest-house and it's all been arranged. Nyree,' something like desperation crept into Gwen's voice, 'won't you consider it?'

Nyree hesitated again.

'You'll have all day tomorrow to arrange things,' Gwen said. 'Not that—I mean for one night . . .' She trailed off uncharacteristically.

Nyree sighed then laughed. 'All right. I hope these are not monster children or something like that, though, Gwen.'

'Why do you say that?'

'Well, you sound . . . I don't know. It just crossed my mind that maybe everyone else on your books has had some experience of them and flatly refused you.'

'I *swear* that is not the case,' Gwen said emphatically.

'OK, OK, I believe you,' Nyree said wryly. 'Give me all the details.'

Looking down at the placid baby in her arms and across at Miss Sarah Waverley, five, and Master Darren Waverley, three, Nyree remembered her words about monster children and smiled to herself. Not only were they bright, happy children but seasoned travellers. In fact their mother had been much more disturbed about this temporary parting than her offspring and had fought to hide her tears at the airport.

'Darling,' her husband had said, 'we'll only be away for three weeks, it will be the trip of a lifetime for you and you know how the kids love your parents and they love them.'

Mrs Waverley, a pretty young blonde, had sniffed, reminded Darren and Sarah to be good to Nanna and Pop, and for the umpteenth time reminded Nyree that Laura, the baby, would be ready for a feed in about two hours. And for a moment it had looked as if she might decide to change places with Nyree when they had been asked to board the Cessna King-Air, but her husband had taken her firmly by the hand. Darren and Sarah had waved excitedly from the plane steps then hopped inside enthusiastically.

And so far, the only thing that hadn't gone according to plan was Laura's feeding time. She had decided politely but firmly to partake of her bottle earlier than her mother had predicted. But now, with less than half an hour of the flight to go, Nyree had also fed Peter and Sarah from the picnic hamper, and herself, and all the children at least were drowsy and contented.

There were no other passengers on the sleek little plane but some freight bound for Mount Isa, she gathered from her conversation with the pilot. It was a charter company that operated the King-Air and these stops at outback stations were common, he had told her. He had also told her that she would have adult company on the flight home tomorrow because he had two passengers to pick up in Mount Isa the following morning before collecting her. Of Niranda Downs, he'd told her that it was a cattle station south of Longreach and that it had been recently sold and renamed, bought by some big company, he thought.

It was a perfect day for flying, beautiful weather, and, as always, much more interesting in a small plane. Nyree stared down at the landscape below, and decided she felt more relaxed than she had for ages despite her reluctance to accept this assignment.

Then the pilot was descending and banking for the landing and the children sat up excitedly although Laura slept on peacefully. In fact she slept right through the landing and only woke when Nyree put her down on a spare seat to help the other two disembark, and straight from sleep she smiled a dazzling smile up at Nyree. 'You're just a poppet!' Nyree said with a grin and tickled her chin to be rewarded by a fat chuckle.

So it was that her first impressions of Niranda Downs were tinged with a feeling of warmth. How could one not be affected by such a gorgeous baby, or for that matter by two happy children delighted to see their grandparents who had been waiting beside the runway next to their Land Rover.

She didn't at first notice much else at all in the excited welter of greetings. 'Oh, look at Laura! Hasn't she grown . . . yes, of course, you've grown too, Darren, and you, Sarah! My, my, you're quite a grown-up young lady . . .' And finally the grandfather said to her, 'No problems, Miss—Westbrook, isn't it?'

'None at all, they were marvellous. Have you got far to drive?'

'Only about an hour. We'll soon have them home and settled in. Thank you so much for looking after them!'

'It was a pleasure,' Nyree said honestly and helped to pack the children's luggage into the Rover. But as the children themselves were being strapped in, she looked around suddenly, for the first time really.

The airstrip was in the centre of a dusty paddock that appeared to stretch as far as the eye could see in all but one direction and there was no other sign of human or any other kind of life. Just the Land Rover and its happy occupants and the plane with the pilot already at the controls again, preparing for take-off. In fact as she watched he gave her a thumbs-up sign and the aircraft began to roll forward.

And for one eerie moment, she visualised herself being stranded in this vast, dusty paddock with the plane flying off in one direction and the Land Rover driving off with its happy load. In fact so strong was the feeling that she felt like running after the plane and begging the pilot to take her to Mount Isa for the night—why hadn't she done that anyway? Or spent it with the Waverley children's grandparents if their home was only an hour's drive away? Why had she consented to being dumped on a vast station among utter strangers . . . why had none of this occurred to her before?

She clenched her fists and felt a dew of sweat break out on her brow, and as the plane gathered speed she turned back convulsively to the Land Rover, but Mrs Waverley's parents were both staring towards a cloud of dust on the short horizon, and just as Nyree was about to speak, a vehicle materialised through the cloud of dust about a mile away.

'There he is,' they said simultaneously and the woman, who was a fair but faded replica of her daughter, added, 'Would you mind if we made tracks, Miss Westbrook? You'll be well looked after, I can assure you, and it's so hot for the little ones in the car.'

Nyree swallowed and unclenched her fists and chided herself for being morbidly fanciful. 'No, of course, not,' she said. 'Goodbye.'

And at the same time as the plane took off, the Land Rover drove away, and she called out again that it had been a pleasure, to their repeated thank-yous.

Then she turned to watch the other vehicle approach and realised that a mile might have been a conservative estimate, because the light was tricky, or perhaps it was a heat haze that now made it look as if it was travelling across a sheet of clear, shiny water.

Whatever, she had the opportunity to feel the fierceness of the sun striking through her thin blue blouse and jeans, to feel her hair, although it was tied back, heavy on her neck and to attract the notorious little bush fly which plagues anything that moves in outback Australia.

Then the car was perceptibly closer and she shaded her eyes and saw that it was a bright yellow Range Rover with something painted on its side in white letters. Something like NYRANDA DOWNS, she thought and frowned. *Nyr*anda? Well, she had never actually seen the name written and the pronunciation could be confused as she well knew from people who called her Niree instead of Nyree.

Where or why the premonition came to her, she was not able to say, and couldn't believe it had anything to do with the first three letters of her name which coincided with the first three letters of the name of this property, but all over again she was gripped by a sense of unease. Only this time it was worse, this time the sweat trickling between her breasts and her shoulder-blades and gathering at her hairline turned stone cold.

And stayed cold as the Range Rover pulled up a few feet away from her and she read the smaller letters beneath the larger legend through the dust ... Matthews & Inchwood.

And her gaze jerked to the driver, now getting out slowly—Reid.

She closed her eyes deliberately and felt the earth tilt beneath her feet, and when they fluttered open Reid had come right up to her and put a hand on her arm—no mirage as she had seen earlier, but Reid in the flesh looming over her, his blue eyes sober and concerned.

Reid saying, 'Nyree? Are you all right?'

Her tongue seemed to want to stick to the roof of her mouth and her eyes to dilate but finally she managed to stammer, 'Oh God—what a coincidence! I'm sorry, I had no idea . . .'

He said, 'It's no coincidence.'

She blinked. 'I don't under*stand*. You mean, somehow or other you . . . engineered this?'

He nodded.

'*Why*?'

'I wanted to see you again—I wanted to put a proposition to you.'

His hand was still on her arm, on the crook of her elbow, and nothing had changed about him that she could see. Not physically. He was still as deeply tanned, still as tall and commanding, but there was something about his aura that was different—then she realised it was the first time she had seen him dressed this way, in a khaki bush shirt and khaki trousers, both faded and mended and obviously working clothes, and brown boots. Gone was the sophisticated aura of a man about town and in its place was a Reid she didn't really know. A man at home in this huge landscape, a man at home with the elements, tough, contained, austere, a man . . . Oh please, she thought, not that old daydream again. And anyway I do know him and perhaps I can guess what he has in mind because . . . well, what else could it be?

'No,' she said hoarsely. 'I'll never be your mistress again. Did you think I *could*? Or if you're thinking of Simon, of another arrangement for his sake, how could you use a child . . . Is he here?' There was real fear in her eyes.

'No.'

Something like relief replaced the fear but she said,

'He should be, surely? It's school holidays . . . oh no, you want me to take him away . . .?'

'Shut up, Nyree,' he said clearly and coldly. 'What the hell do you take me for?'

'I don't know,' she whispered. 'I don't know but you shouldn't have done this. You shouldn't have . . .'

'Don't you even want to know what I'm doing here?' he queried sardonically.

'No . . . What does it matter? Oh *hell*! I knew I should have gone on that plane. I just had this intuition,' she said wildly. 'How can I get off this place?'

He stared down at her, taking in her sudden pallor and the sheen of tears in her eyes, the way her lips worked, the state she was in.

'You can't,' he said at last. 'At least, not until tomorrow morning. Not unless I choose to fly you myself, which I don't.'

'*Reid*,' she sucked in a desperate breath, 'the last thing I want to hear is any propositions from you. It's *over*. I . . . all right, once upon a time I thought it might take the course of those books you read, that you'd marry me for Simon's sake and end up falling in love with me—I even thought I might do it but that . . . that seems half a lifetime away,' she said hollowly. 'I know now I couldn't, I don't want to, I'm worth more than that. Don't you remember—*you* made me see it!'

'Are you committed to anyone else?' he asked tautly, and added ironically, 'As a result of what I made you see?'

'Com . . . no.' She tilted her head back proudly and anger glittered in her green eyes. 'Isn't that hitting below the belt?' she asked scornfully.

He shrugged. 'If you like. But it might also be a good reason to check out what I have to offer,' he said emotionlessly. 'You could find yourself surprised.'

'Surprised,' she repeated, hopelessly and helplessly. 'No. I think I know you too well.'

'Oddly enough, I don't think you know me at all well,' he said grimly. 'But we don't have to stand *here* debating this. Get in.' He released her arm and bent to pick up her overnight bag which he tossed into the back seat. Then he put a hand on her arm again to lead her around to the passenger door but she shook him off—and could have killed him for the sudden speculative gleam in his eye which said so clearly— afraid of my touching you, Nyree?

But it was obvious that she had no choice but to go with him.

They didn't have far to go.

The near horizon was in fact the lip of a fold in the landscape, and the track from the airfield led down a gradual slope to almost a different world. In fact it wasn't so much a fold in the ground she saw, but a lower, smaller plateau set into the side of the higher one, and with a breathtaking view of miles and miles of plain below. But it was green in patches with trees growing around depressions, dams or natural lakes, she guessed. There were cattle-yards and windmills, buildings, people, horses.

In any other circumstances she would have been astonished and delighted by this revelation. As it was all she could do was sit stiffly upright as far away as possible from Reid, blinking surreptitiously because to cry would be the ultimate weakness.

But he drove slowly down the track and along the winding dirt road so she could not help but take some of it in.

Then he pulled up at last before a sprawling old homestead, surrounded by ghost gums and paper-barks, a house with wide verandas all around, in good repair and fresh paint with several tall brick chimneys and a thick green lawn around it—and a brand-new-looking tennis court beside it. A house set away from the other buildings and the cattle yards.

Reid got out, collected her bag and his wide-brimmed hat which had also been on the back seat, and came round to open her door for her.

She climbed down avoiding his gaze and stared around. Then she said abruptly. 'Who lives here? Is this the guest-house?'

'No. I do. Come in.'

She hesitated, but he didn't wait for her, so she reluctantly climbed the verdanda steps behind him. But she did say, '*Is* there a guest-house?'

'Oh, yes,' he glanced over his shoulder and she saw the amusement in his eyes before he added, 'I'll tell you about it. Would you like to wash? Change, perhaps? It's past lunch time but we could have some tea.'

They were standing opposite the front door which was heavily panelled with a huge brass knob but open, and through it she could see a long passageway, tiled with green and white squares that stretched right through to the back of the house. The walls were papered in a soft matt green paper to match the green tiles and the ornate wooden door surrounds along it, enamelled in white. A typical old 'Queenslander', she thought, with the central passageway bisecting the house—living-quarters one side, sleeping-quarters the other and all the rooms with high ceilings, making them cool, and the veranda around helping to counteract the fierce heat of summer. But most of them with fireplaces as well because by contrast the nights could be cold. A practical yet elegant old house, she thought—a gem.

She rubbed her face uncertainly and discovered it felt gritty with dust. 'A . . . wash, thanks, yes,' she said huskily.

He led her down the passage and through a doorway into a bedroom and put her bag down on the bed. 'The bathroom is through there,' he said quietly, indicating another door. 'I'll put the kettle on. Just yell out if you get lost.' And he left her.

Lost, she thought with despair.

The bathroom had been modernised, and showed no sign of having been used recently. At least there was nothing in it to denote that anyone used it regularly, just two fluffy chrysanthemum-yellow towels to match the gleaming new porcelain of the bath and basin against white walls and floor. She thought absently, as she opened her toilet bag and inspected herself in the mirror, that the bedroom it led off had the same look— a pleasant, chintzy spare bedroom, with new carpet, also chrysanthemum-yellow, new curtains, new bedspread, flowered yellow on white, and some beautiful old furniture.

And she frowned at her reflection, unable to piece together her impressions of this marvellous old house or, as in the case of Reid himself earlier, to judge its aura.

She sighed and forced herself to concentrate on refreshing herself. After she had washed her face and hands, she sprayed a fresh citrusy cologne on to her skin and smoothed a light moisturiser on to her face. Then she untied her hair and brushed it vigorously and left it loose. She shaped her eyebrows absently, straightened the collar of her blouse and was about to turn away from the shadows she saw in her eyes, but stopped and forced herself to look herself squarely in the face. For heaven's sake, don't let him see them, Nyree, she warned, but immediately wondered if he hadn't already.

Then she replaced her toilet gear in her bag, strapped on her watch and left the bedroom.

She crossed the passage and entered one of the only two doorways on the other side, coming into a huge room with a fireplace at each end and a wooden arch spanning the middle. A lounge-cum-dining-room probably, she thought, with french windows leading off it on to the veranda. But it was completely unfurnished. Newly carpeted in a very close pile, fine wool, sandy pink with matching wallpaper and white woodwork, but not one piece of furniture.

She stared around, thinking what a wonderful room it would be to furnish with its high, white, pressed-iron ceiling divided by the arch, but she caught her thoughts deliberately and crossed to one of the french windows. The veranda was wide with honey-stained floorboards, a half-wall with a wide ledge and a set of curving stone steps leading to a flagged, flower-bordered path that in turn led across the grass to the tennis court.

She turned away with a sudden lump in her throat and jumped, because Reid was standing behind her and she hadn't heard him.

'The kitchen is this way,' he said and she followed him down the room to a door leading to the back of the house, down a short passage and into a bright, airy, old-fashioned kitchen.

There were tea things set out on the big table in the middle of the room and a plate of biscuits from a packet. He pulled out a chair for her and she sat down. And he was silent, pouring the tea while she looked around, noting the wood-burning stove as well as an electric one, the enormous refrigerator-freezer and the separate room, as big as her kitchen, that was the pantry.

Then she realised her tea was in front of her and he was offering her a biscuit. She shook her head.

'Have some tea then,' he advised. 'You look as if you could do with it.'

She flinched inwardly but picked up her cup and glanced at him through her lashes over the rim. But he wasn't looking at her, he was selecting a biscuit and she lowered her lashes and sipped her tea, but it was too hot so she put her cup down and looked around helplessly again.

The silence lengthened uncomfortably until every nerve she possessed seemed to be tuned to screaming point.

Then he said, 'Well, what do you think if it?'

Her eyes flew to his before she could stop herself. 'I . . .' She licked her lips and took another sip of tea to steady herself. 'I think it's lovely,' she said very quietly but sincerely.

'Can I tell you about it?'

'If . . . if you want to.'

'Oh, I do—I'd like to do three things, Nyree. I'd like to tell you about it, show you some of it and then discuss the . . . theory of it with you. Perhaps that's a better word than the one I used before. All I ask is that you hear me out, no more, so you don't have to be afraid of anything. Will you do that?'

'Reid, all right, I'll hear you out—I don't have much choice—but . . .'

'Just wait until I've finished, Nyree,' he said drily. Then he moved his wide shoulders more comfortably against the back of the chair, fiddled with his spoon, stared past her briefly then captured her gaze compellingly, and said abruptly, 'I own this place in partnership with Harold—and to a lesser extent, the bank. We bought it several months ago—we hadn't planned to but it came on the market unexpectedly, and I found myself making an equally unexpected decision. Which, in part, was that I was tired of my lifestyle, that Matthews & Inchwood were firmly enough established for me to play less of a direct role, that I could turn my attention to something else, although something related. And I suddenly remembered all those years as a kid when I'd dreamed of owning my own cattle station. Those were *some* of my reasons,' he said with an odd sort of emphasis.

'I . . .' She stopped.

He raised an eyebrow at her.

'I was going to say that I think you started to mention once that your life-style was . . . but we were interrupted. Go on.'

He studied her silently for a moment. Then he said, 'Yes, I was, by a mouse to be precise.' But there was no amusement in his blue eyes, only a brooding sombreness. 'Anyway,' he said presently, 'we bought it, I moved in and I've done some renovations, mainly to this house, but otherwise concentrated my energies on cattle, but this time from a personal point of view. I've become a grazier first and foremost but of course it's very handy to be a vet as well. And eventually, Matthews & Inchwood will benefit. We'll be able to hold seminars here with our own herd as, hopefully, show-piece cattle. By the way, that's what the guest-house will be for. But that's at least a year off.'

'And how many people do you employ?' she asked with a spark of genuine interest despite herself.

'There are about a dozen actually living here. Two families each with several children apiece and then the single hands. Then there's myself, occasionally Harold and Amanda and of course, there'll be Simon.'

'So,' Nyree looked around again at the homely, neat kitchen, 'how do you manage?'

'One of the wives "does" for me.'

'It must be a very different life,' she whispered.

'Oh, it is.' Their gazes locked and held. Then he said, 'Would you like to see some more of it?'

'I . . . yes.'

* * *

It was a fairly brief guided tour he took her on in the yellow Range Rover. He showed her the helipad with a blue and white helicopter sitting on it. He showed her the staff accommodation—compact bungalows, some with gardens. He showed her the station farm with its small herd of dairy cattle, chickens, ducks and turkeys, and three children rushed out of the milking-shed to wave enthusiastically as they drove by. They passed the stables and a weather-beaten man with the bowed legs of someone who had spent half his life in a saddle. Indeed, he had just dismounted as they saw him.

'That's Lefty Hancock,' Reid said with a grin. 'He's lived here all his life and is the spinner of the tallest tales I've ever heard.'

But Lefty doffed his hat with the utmost courtesy and Nyree smiled and waved.

Then Reid drove back to the homestead but instead of taking her in, he said, 'Come and see this.'

She followed him round the side of the house and down the path that, once beyond the garden perimeter, wound through scrub and began to climb towards the rocky wall that led to the airfield plateau above. It wasn't a difficult climb but it was hot in the late afternoon sunlight, and Nyree wiped her brow, then frowned as she thought she heard running water. But the foliage was thick and the light dim and the sound muffled beneath a canopy of interwoven branches, and she was just wondering if she had imagined it when she breasted a rise and came out into the sunlight and she gasped at the scene that lay before her.

A rock pool beneath a cascading waterfall, a pool the size of two tennis courts at the base of a cliff surrounded by trees and boulders and hanging vines, a pool of clear, sparkling jade-green water, incredibly inviting.

'Oh!' she breathed. 'I don't believe it.'

'I didn't either at first,' Reid said. 'I thought it was a mirage.'

'But—does the water always run?' She looked up at the narrow, glittering cascade. 'How . . .?'

'It's part of a system of underground springs, apparently,' he said. 'A system that has never completely dried up in living memory. Come.' He held out a hand and she put hers into it unthinkingly.

He led her across the rocks to a large smooth, weathered one partly shaded by the overhanging limb of a gum tree. And from it across the pool, you could see through the trees to the plain below.

'This is my favourite spot. Could we sit down here a while?'

She could only acquiesce, still drinking in the beauty of the spot.

They sat side by side on the rock in silence for a time. Then he said, 'The real reason I bought this place was because of a dream, a daydream, *your* daydream.'

Nyree had been staring at the view, shading her eyes with her hand, but she dropped her hand and turned to him with her eyes widening and her lips parted.

'And that's what I meant when I said I wanted to put a proposition to you, Nyree,' he said quietly, studying her parted lips for a moment then raising his blue gaze to her incredulous green one. 'I suppose you could call it a scientific proposition in a sense. For example, take a man like myself, a man with a failed marriage behind him—and then if that wasn't traumatic enough, finding he had a son he'd never known about. Enough to make him a bit wary of women, probably don't you agree?'

'Yes. Yes, I do understand that,' she said in a low husky voice.

'All right, but let's take his case further. He thinks then in a twisted kind of way, that it's all behind him apart from the son, but that's an unexpected bonus, and now he has the best of both worlds. Continuity of himself, women when he wants them but no ties, no . . . drama, no possibility of getting caught again, lied to, cheated.' He stopped and shrugged. 'He wasn't really very bright, this man. Because when the best thing that had ever happened to him came into his life, he did his best to run away from it and then . . . well, you know what happened then, don't you, Nyree?' he said quietly but compelling.

'Reid . . .' Her voice shook.

'But to continue,' he said levelly although he put out a hand and picked up one of hers, 'although this . . . fool tried to cling to his cynicism, he began to think strangely and act strangely. He became obsessed by a dream, someone else's but one that woke the same desires within him. And while he couldn't exactly duplicate this dream, not the place nor the time, he did think he'd . . . achieved the essence of it. He bought a property where he thought he and his . . . co-dreamer could share a life together . . . as they'd dreamed of. He even partly named it after her. Do you, speaking scientifically, have any theory about what happened to this man, Nyree?'

She could only stare at him helplessly, breathing erratically as if she had been running.

'I do,' he said, grasping her hand tighter. 'I believe he fell in love, perhaps for the first time ever, so very much in love that he couldn't help himself, desperately in love with his . . . co-dreamer. But unfortunately, the things he'd said and the things he'd done had damaged his credibility and this was the one way he thought he could *prove* to her how he felt. By presenting her with the facts of it. Does that make any sense to you, Nyree?'

His eyes searched hers, green as the pool beside them and sparkling with tears. 'Oh, Reid . . .' she whispered but he interrupted her.

'Let me say it all. I . . .' his voice was curiously unsteady now, 'there was another factor that made me want to present you with a *fait accompli*. Simon—I didn't want there ever to be any misunderstandings about that. I love you, Nyree, for yourself. If there was no Simon it wouldn't make the slightest difference to me. I love you and I need you and I want to marry you. But, I have to warn you that some of that fool lived on in me even after I'd realised what was happening to me—perhaps it always will. That night,' he said with an effort, 'I'd come to present you with the facts. I'd come to say basically what I've said now—only to see you with another man and become possessed by a rage of jealousy and insanity. Not to mention a sudden lack of confidence . . .'

Her lips quivered. 'There was *nothing* . . .'

'I know . . .'

'You didn't believe me then.'

He sighed. 'It must be something to do with being in love—it's crazy. I believe in you more than anyone I've ever known. But *then*, I don't know how to describe it—all I could think was . . . of you wanting to be with someone else, and cursing myself for how dreadfully it mattered to me, and cursing myself for being so taken up with my own feelings that I might have misjudged yours. I was a fool, a mad fool too much in love to see straight. But you . . .' He stopped and that nerve beat suddenly in his jaw.

'I lied,' she whispered. 'Out of anger, hurt and because I'm a fool, I lied. Oh Reid, hold me,' she begged, 'because the truth of the matter is—it only took me four days to fall in love with you and I've never stopped but I was also wary and . . . trying to protect myself from being hurt again.'

He held her so hard for a time, she could barely breathe. Then he released her but kept hold of her hand and said intently, 'If only you knew how much I've missed you and hated myself.'

'If only you knew how much I've missed you and been in utter despair. In fact if it hadn't been for Miss Hambro, and to a lesser extent my aunt . . .' She smiled through her tears.

'Then you believe me and you can forgive me?' he queried.

'How could I not?' she said simply.

Even to be with Reid was the last thing Nyree had visualised when she had left Brisbane that morning. To be staring into his eyes and seeing the relief and the love in them was a possibility that had not remotely occurred to her, and it was with a curious feeling of unreality that she raised unsteady fingers to smooth the lines beside his mouth. He caught her wrist and kissed the palm of her hand. She slipped her free hand beneath the collar of his shirt and they stayed like that for a time.

Then he said unsteadily, 'I once made a rather offensive remark to you about making love in the bush—but at least this isn't beside a public pathway as you very correctly pointed out, and I'm afraid the boot is on the other foot this time, my darling.'

'Oh?' she said huskily, a smile tugging at her lips.

'Well,' he amended, 'when I say that it's not quite true. You were never very keen on the idea but this time, I just don't think I have the strength to leave this place without making love to you. Would it offend you very much?' His hand moved on her cheek. 'There's a bed of soft grass just behind us and I think—it seems to me anyway, it's there just for us.'

'Oh, I think . . .' she murmured and stopped.

'What?' he prompted softly.

'It would be very proper.'

His lips twisted into a smile. 'You have changed, my Amazon.'

'It's all your doing, Mr Matthews,' she said gravely.

'I never wanted to change you—that's why I love you, because you're . . . you.'

'You wanted to change me then,' she whispered.

'I wanted to . . . tame you,' he said wryly. 'I wanted to think of you submitting in a . . . properly feminine manner. I've come a long way . . . to this.'

'So have I, as you noted just now. I'm ready and

willing and waiting to ... submit in a properly feminine manner,' she said with tears shimmering in her eyes. 'It's very strange, isn't it? It must be love.'

'Then you really don't mind if I do this,' he fiddled with the buttons of her blouse, 'here?'

'No, I really don't.' Her blouse came open and she helped him to take it off her, and then her bra. 'I think it has a special sort of significance,' she said softly as the straps slid down her arms and her breasts were released. 'Don't you?'

He raised his eyes to hers at last. 'Yes ... oh God, Nyree, I must warn you I want you desperately, I've dreamt about you and these,' he lifted his hands and stroked her nipples, 'and not only in my sleep. Most of my waking moments until I thought I'd go mad. I ... I'm telling you this, my love, because in a moment or two I'm likely to lose all control, just warning you what to expect because you look a little dazed ...'

'I ... I'm also ...' She abandoned speech because the truth was she *was* dazed but full to the brim with love for him, lost for words except for a bare few. 'Love me please, Reid.'

The grass was soft as he had predicted, and lush and green and the sunlight filtered. And his arms were strong and his desire for her, a driving, loving need ... as he had also predicted. But it drew a response from her that was as untamed, as free, as momentous as his loving.

And they lay exhausted for a long time in each other's arms afterwards. But, as their strength returned, Nyree experienced some reaction—an unwillingness to leave his arms, although he showed no desire to let her go, other signs . . .

'It is like a dream,' she murmured shakily, kissing his shoulder as the sun slipped down the sky and a flock of white corellas circled the tree tops.

'No, this is reality, my darling,' he corrected. 'Did I hurt you?'

'No. Why?'

'You're crying,' he said softly and kissed her eyelids.

'I'm crying for joy and because this morning, well, I never expected . . .' A tremor shook her body. 'I so nearly didn't accept this job—imagine . . .'

'Shh . . .' He stroked her hair. 'I would have come. Mrs Foster was only the first string to my bow.'

'She knew? I don't understand.'

'I'll explain—Jim and Mary Whittaker, the couple who picked up their grandchildren from you today, came over to see me in a great state of excitement a few days ago. Their daughter and son-in-law—well you know all that, but they wanted to know if it would be all right to use the airstrip and I said yes, of course. Then they mentioned that unless someone could be found to accompany the children, Mary would have to fly down and pick them up. I . . . it was like a revelation to me,' he said huskily. 'I had a sudden vision of you and I knew that I couldn't go on any longer without seeing you. That in all my brooding and isolation of the past weeks one thing had been niggling at the back of my mind—I'd never told you I loved you, and how could I expect anything in return when I'd never done that?

'So, I recommended Mrs Foster's agency, I even

recommended you by name and told them about Simon's holiday and how marvellous you'd been. They were thrilled and determined to have you and nobody but you escort their precious cargo up here. But to be on the safe side, I rang Gwen Foster myself and swore her to secrecy—I told her briefly about us.'

'I *thought* she sounded odd but I couldn't put my finger on it,' Nyree said.

'And you had no presentiments?'

'Not really until we'd landed. Then I got this strangest feeling . . . And then when you drove up, before I saw you, I saw the name on the side of the Range Rover.'

'Ah that,' he said. 'I wondered if it might give you a clue. It's actually a contraction of Nyree and Amanda.'

'Nyranda,' Nyree said slowly. 'So they know? Harold and Amanda?'

'Curiously enough, Amanda guessed there was something between us on Keppel. Yes, they know . . . Nyree,' his voice changed, becoming more serious, 'I must warn you, going into beef cattle is . . . well, beef prices fluctuate, there's no guaranteeing world markets, this part of the world is notorious for either drought or flood. Not that Harold and I haven't gone into it all thoroughly but it's still a challenge . . .'

'I wouldn't want it to be any other way,' she whispered. 'Does Simon—no . . .'

'No. I can't imagine that it won't come as anything but the best news to him now, though. He loves it up here, by the way. I was going down to Brisbane tomorrow to spend a few days and then to bring him back. Will you come with me?'

She didn't have to answer.

'We could even invite Miss Hambro up for holidays,' Reid said. 'Think she'd like that?'

'More than anything—what's the mouse situation up here?'

They laughed together.

'Know what I'd like to do now?' he said presently.

'No.'

'Take you for a swim. Come . . .'

The water was surprisingly fresh considering the heat of the day and they swam naked. It was a new experience for Nyree and it affected her deeply—to be so marvellously free, in their own world with the sun setting and gilding their wet, gleaming bodies, to have Reid lifting her up to admire the way the water streamed off her breasts, then burying his head between them as they fell back into it. Only to come up again, their bodies entwined, their hair sleek and dripping, her arms wound about his neck, kissing each other deeply . . .

They stayed in the water until it was all but dark then had to put their clothes on with difficulty because they had nothing to dry themselves with.

So that as soon as they reached the homestead, Reid said it was only practical to get undressed again; after all, their clothes were damp now too and wasn't that a way to catch a chill?

She agreed gravely and submitted to being towelled down intimately then laid on his big bed—still unclothed.

'Is this no way to catch a chill?' she asked as he lay down beside her.

'Definitely not—the opposite,' he murmured, barely hesitating in his self-appointed task of keeping her warm. In other words, stroking her breasts, plucking her nipples then cupping them in his palms, taking time off to make sure that no other part of her smooth, soft, fresh body was neglected by his hands or his lips. 'It's a great way to *avoid* being chilled in fact, don't you think?'

'I think you're having me on,' she teased. 'But chills aside,' she added, 'isn't this a way to become old before our time?'

'No,' he said intensely. 'The way for me to get old, I've discovered, is to be without you. Not to be able to do this.' His hand moved to the small of her back then caressed the curve of her bottom and finally came to rest on her inner thigh where her skin was like pearly silk, and so sensitive that her whole body trembled at his touch. 'Like that?' he asked barely audibly.

'Love it,' she whispered, her lips curving into a secret little smile.

'I know why you're laughing at me,' he said wryly. 'You're thinking that you always were way ahead of me.'

Her smile widened and she pushed her fingers through his damp hair. 'Oh, way ahead,' she agreed softly and slid her fingers down the side of his face to touch his mouth, outline it with one finger.

'And you're feeling better now?' he said softly, drawing her body closer.

'I *was* feeling . . . how did you know?' she asked.

'I've seen victims of shock before.' Something grim flickered briefly in his eyes then he buried his head in her hair and said with an effort, 'I'm sorry—I'd give anything to be able to undo these past weeks.'

'Oh, Reid,' she clung to him, 'but we know so much more now, don't we? It has to be even better now, deeper, wider, forged through the hard times as well as the good. Although,' her voice cracked a little but when he lifted his head it was to see her green eyes filled with love and laughter, 'right now I'm not only warm but positively, well . . . hot. You might have to take responsibility for that, my darling.'

He did, but this time with gentleness and great care.

Harlequin Presents

Coming Next Month

1103 MISTRESS OF PILLATORO Emma Darcy
Crushed by a broken love affair, Jessica welcomes Gideon Cavilha's offer to research his father's historical theories. Once at Pillatoro, his magnificent family estate, she feels strangely as if she belonged. But her one chance of staying there depends on her telling a lie!

1104 SMOKE IN THE WIND Robyn Donald
Six years ago Ryan Fraine had taken over Venetia's life and shattered it. And he had chosen her cousin instead. Now, though he still seems to want her, and Venetia feels he's entitled to know his son, she's too proud to be second choice....

1105 SUBSTITUTE LOVER Penny Jordan
Stephanie never told Gray Chalmers the truth about her marriage to his cousin, Paul. And she's avoided the town where he and Paul ran a boatyard and Paul accidentally died. Now Gray needs her help and she owes him so much. Can she return and face the memories?

1106 OUT OF CONTROL Charlotte Lamb
Marooned in her fogbound cottage with a particularly infuriating man, Liza's well-ordered emotions—scarred by an adolescent indiscretion—threaten to break down. Yet she's determined to resist G. K. Gifford's dangerous attraction, sure that, to him, it's all just a game....

1107 CLOSE COLLABORATION Leigh Michaels
Mallory's first meeting with sociologist C. Duncan Adams leaves little hope that he'll help with her cherished project. The trouble starts immediately, long before she finds out about the woman in his life, and he learns about the men in hers....

1108 A PAINFUL LOVING Margaret Mayo
Everyone on the Greek island of Lakades thinks Aleko Tranakas is the perfect antidote for a young widow's loneliness. Not Kara. She doesn't want an affair, especially with a practiced womanizer whose seductive charms remind her of her husband. She won't make that mistake again!

1109 ULTIMATUM Sally Wentworth
Powerboat racing is the strong passion of Reid Lomax's life. Casey's fear is equally strong—that she'll lose her newlywed husband in an accident. So she presents him with an ultimatum that she thinks he can't ignore....

1110 A MOMENT OF ANGER Patricia Wilson
Nick Orsiani is a man accustomed to getting what he wants, and what he wants now is Rachel. Rachel, however, soon initiates a plan of her own—a dangerous, winner-take-all contest!

Available in September wherever paperback books are sold, or through Harlequin Reader Service:

In the U.S.
901 Fuhrmann Blvd.
P.O. Box 1397
Buffalo, N.Y. 14240-1397

In Canada
P.O. Box 603
Fort Erie, Ontario
L2A 5X3

Temptation™

TEMPTATION WILL BE
EVEN HARDER TO RESIST...

In September, Temptation is presenting a sophisticated new face to the world. A fresh look that truly brings Harlequin's most intimate romances into focus.

What's more, all-time favorite authors Barbara Delinsky, Rita Clay Estrada, Jayne Ann Krentz and Vicki Lewis Thompson will join forces to help us celebrate. The result? A very special quartet of Temptations...

- **Four striking covers**
- **Four stellar authors**
- **Four sensual love stories**
- **Four variations on one spellbinding theme**

All in one great month! Give in to Temptation in September.

TDESIGN-1

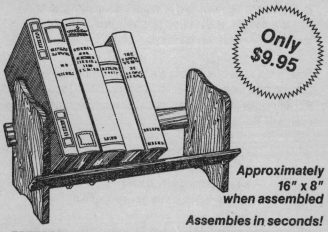

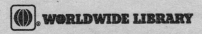

Harlequin Intrigue

Two exciting new stories each month.

Each title mixes a contemporary, sophisticated romance with the surprising twists and turns of a puzzler...romance with "something more."

Because romance can be quite an adventure.

Intrg-1

Romance, Suspense and Adventure